Unforeseen

M.C. DECKER

Heather,
Embrace the
Unforeseen!
XXOO
M.C. Decker

Cover Design:
Michele Catalano, Michele Catalano Creative
www.michelecatalanocreative.com

Interior Design and Formatting:
Christine Borgford, Type A Formatting
www.typeAformatting.com

Cover photos:
Lauren Perry, Perrywinkle Photography
www.perrywinklephotography.com

Dedication

To those who've suffered through the hardest goodbye; May life's unforeseen events lead you to another chance at your happily-ever-after.

Prologue

Goodbye (noun): an instance of saying "goodbye"; a parting. "A final goodbye."
One word. Two syllables. Both so finite.
We'd both said our fair share of goodbyes throughout our lives. Why did this one seem the most difficult?

BLAKE ~ *December 2012*

*A*S THE LIMOUSINE driver chauffeured us through the city and out to the country cemetery, I repeated the words I'd prepared in hopes of giving my wife–the love of my life and mother of my children—a proper goodbye. It was rather ironic considering we'd never believed in goodbyes.

After several weeks of studying media law together, I'd finally convinced Alyssa to go out on a proper date. Honestly, it was probably more due to the fact that I was worried about my buddy Rich swooping in and stealing her away from me. To my relief, she agreed and after a romantic evening filled with laughter and deep conversation, I was here standing with her at her doorstep.

"I had a great time tonight, Blake," she said, staring up into my eyes. "I hope we can do this again sometime."

"We will most definitely be doing this again soon," I responded, pulling her in tightly against my chest. Feeling her heartbeat quicken with my touch, I knew she wanted to kiss me just as much as I wanted a taste of her. Maybe I was being too forward for just the first date, but I couldn't control my impulses. I'd been imagining the taste of her lips

on mine ever since she'd first pulled out a tube of cherry lip gloss on the first day of class.

Even wearing stilettos, Alyssa stood on her tiptoes as I pulled her in for our first kiss–our lips parted, our tongues danced, and our breathing became one. In that moment, I knew I never wanted another first kiss. This woman would become my wife—my first, my last, my everything.

After what seemed like an eternity, we drew away. The electricity between us still enough to spark a flame.

"I think I should probably say goodbye before I end up doing something that I may regret later," I rasped.

"Never goodbye, Blake. It may sound silly, but I've never believed in goodbyes. I don't want us to ever have to say it. But, you're right—I think before I act impulsively, I probably should say good night and I'll see you later," Alyssa whispered, her warm breath dancing across my cheek.

Smiling at her words, I knew she was right. I responded by placing a chaste kiss on her cheek. "I agree. Never goodbye just good night and I'll see you later, Short Stack," I said with a wink.

She smiled and swatted at me for the use of the nickname I'd given her on the day we'd met several weeks earlier.

"Never goodbye," I whispered to myself, as she turned and stepped into her apartment building.

But, as I'd learned, the universe sometimes had other plans for us.

I gazed out the window as the blur of the city lights turned to rolling hills. The sound of my daughter's laughter claimed my attention. Not even quite a year old, she didn't have any idea the significance of this day–her mother's final goodbye.

Dressed in bright pink, just as my wife would have wanted, I watched as my daughter played with her favorite stuffed dog. I stared into Maddy's crystal-clear, blue eyes, her little orbs reminding me so much of Alyssa's, and wished for a moment that I could transfer all my memories of Alyssa to our daughter.

As hard as this week had been on me, the most difficult part was the heavy realization that our daughter–and now our son— would grow up without knowing their mother's love. And, boy, did she love them both something fierce.

"Blake, it's not too late to call the doctor's office and tell them we changed our minds," Alyssa said, as I opened the passenger door to help her out of the car. We'd just left the doctor's office where my wife had her twenty-week ultrasound. The doctor had informed us that he could tell us the baby's gender, but we'd already agreed to keep it a surprise. Now as we were about to enter the baby boutique, I could tell Alyssa was already starting to question our decision.

"Look at this beautiful pink bedding," she sighed, running her hand across the plush fabric. "I just don't know if I like these neutral colors."

"You don't really want to know, Lys. The surprise will be so worth it once you're holding our son or daughter in your arms."

"I suppose you're right," she said, scrunching her nose up in the most adorable way. The simple gesture alone had me reaching for my cell. It's a good thing the doctor's number wasn't on speed dial, or Alyssa wouldn't have been able to stop me. I'd be a screwed man if our child got that trait from their mother.

"Blake, stop!" she nearly screamed, reaching for my phone. "I don't really want to know. I mean I do, but I don't. Jesus, I don't know what I want," she said, tears beginning to well in her eyes.

"Short Stack, don't cry, Babe," I said, enveloping her in my arms.

"You know I hate it when you call me that," she laughed through her sniffles.

"I know you do, but I love it and I knew it would make you laugh. I think it worked," I smiled, drawing her in for a gentle kiss right in the middle of the store. I wanted my wife to know that I adored her and all of her hormonal quirks, and I didn't care who witnessed our public display of affection.

"I'm sorry I'm so hormonal."

"You're carrying my baby. I think it's acceptable," I said, giving her one last peck on the forehead before pulling away. "Now, let's do some shopping!"

"I like the sound of that! I already see the cutest stuffed dog over there. It would be perfect for our little boy or girl," she said, her blue eyes beaming.

"Blake, we're here," my mother-in-law's voice breaking me from my thoughts. She patted me on the knee and I gave her a knowing nod. It was time and neither of us were ready.

After the chauffeur came and opened the car door, I exited and offered my hand to Judith. She pulled a black veil over her face, probably trying to mask her swollen eyes and puffy cheeks. In that moment, I wished I could hide from the world as well. As much as people didn't want to stare, it was only human nature to watch from afar as I grieved my wife–the only love of my life.

I walked Judith to the graveside and returned to pull Maddy from her car seat. Something in my peripheral vision caught my eye, and it was then that I noticed my best friend Rich's fiancée, Brooke, drop to her knees. Alyssa and Brooke had become good friends since Rich introduced her to us over a year ago. They'd been friends in college and reconnected after several years when she applied for a position at the *Post* where Rich worked.

Before losing their baby, Brooke and Alyssa had both been pregnant at the same time, and the two bonded over talks of morning sickness and prenatal vitamins.

Although I knew Rich and his woman had a long road ahead of them, and many serious discussions in their future, I was able to find a tiny bit of peace in knowing that my turmoil and tragedy brought the two of them back together. I'd always been man enough to admit that I knew what love was, and I was confident that those two had found it.

Some people live their entire life without finding their soul mate. I was certain mine had already come and gone. That part of my heart would always be reserved for Alyssa, and although I was still fairly young, I didn't have any interest in finding love again and I doubted that I ever would.

Perspiration dripped from my forehead as I waited on Alyssa's doorstep. It wasn't even that hot out, and here I was sweating like a pig who'd just run a marathon. This wasn't the impression I was hoping for tonight. I'd been planning this night for months. I wanted everything to be perfect, a night that we'd reminisce about over dinner on our fiftieth wedding anniversary. Most importantly, I wanted her to say "yes."

The door slowly opened and Alyssa's head popped out from the other side.

"You're early! You're never early!" she laughed. "I'm not quite ready yet. Give me two minutes to run back to the bedroom, and then let yourself in."

"Babe, I've seen you naked before. I think you can let me in!" I chuckled, nudging the door open to reveal my girl standing there wearing nothing but a black lace bra and matching panties.

"Blake! I told you to wait!" she said, covering her chest with her arms and scrunching her nose in displeasure.

"You know you're adorable when you act mad at me, right? I said, drawing her in closer.

"I'm not playing!" she pouted. "I really wanted you to wait."

"I couldn't wait another minute without seeing you," I said, placing a gentle kiss on her forehead.

The scowl on her face faded as she relaxed into my chest. "I really should go get ready, or I'll end up with even less clothes on, and I'll never want to leave."

"I think I'd actually be OK with that."

"You are not!" she said, swatting my arm. "You told me that you were taking me someplace special tonight. I bought a new dress and everything and I plan on wearing it!"

"Fine, I'd hate to come between a woman and her new dress. But, hurry because I'm already in the mood for dessert," I said with a wink.

I'd hardly had time to turn on SportsCenter when Alyssa opened the door to the bedroom, calling my name.

"Blake, I can't get my dress zipped. Do you think you can help me?"

My dick swelled in my pants with just the silky sound of her voice. I quickly stood and walked slowly toward the bedroom—like a lion stalking its prey. She stood in the doorway, her back to me. She'd already stepped into a pair of bright red heels. My eyes traveled up her body, stopping right above the swell of her ass where the zipper of the dress taunted me. Instead of covering up her beautiful body, I wanted nothing more than to remove the damn dress. Who the fuck cares if it's new? It belongs in a heap on the floor—along with her bra and panties. She can keep the shoes on, though. Because fuck, those are hot.

"Are you sure I actually have to zip this up? I think it'd be better off," I whispered across her neck.

I couldn't see her face, but I knew I was affecting her.

We never did make our dinner reservations that night, and her new dress did end up in a heap on the floor. I did, however, ask her to marry me—as we were both lying in bed, tangled in the sheets. It may not have turned out to be the night I'd spent months planning—but it was better than anything I could've envisioned. It may not be the ideal, or G-rated story to tell our children, but all that really matters is that she said, "yes."

Chapter One

*L*OOKING DOWN AT my watch, I saw we only had about twenty minutes to make it to the church in time for the rehearsal. The one thing I'd prided myself most on throughout the years in my business as a wedding planner was my punctuality. And, here I was, the maid-of-honor in my best friend's wedding, and we were going to be late.

Barging in to Brooke's bedroom, I saw her staring at her reflection in the mirror–unshed tears rimming her eyes.

"I never thought I'd find you in here on the verge of tears. Now, get it together before you ruin your makeup! We don't have time to redo it," I laughed, rolling my eyes.

"Shut up! Just because you don't believe in showing any emotion doesn't mean the rest of us can't."

"That's not true. I believe in showing my emotional side," I argued.

"Right," she said, eyeing me suspiciously.

"I do! I just learned as a kid that you showed enough for both of us," I sassed back.

"I hate you," she laughed.

"No, you don't. You love me."

"I do," she sighed, once again giving into my charm.

"Now, are you almost ready to go? I just got a text from Rich and everyone is already at the church. Your groom is growing impatient."

"Ha! Well we can't have that now," she said. "I think I'm ready. Do I look OK?"

"Are you kidding me? Twirl around and let me see you! You're stunning, Brookie. You seriously look better than most of my brides, and it's not even your wedding day."

"Shut up! You're only saying that because you're my best friend, but I love you for it."

"You may be my best friend, but everyone else pays me to say it. So, look on the bright side, at least you get my compliments for free," she said with a shrug.

"I'd hardly call the ten bottles of vintage chardonnay you got as payment for maid-of-honor duties as free," she quipped.

"You know you'll drink half!" I said, shaking my head. "Seriously, get your shoes! We need to go!"

Making it to the church with just minutes to spare before the rehearsal was set to begin, Brooke walked into the vestibule ahead of me. Out of the corner of my eye, I saw Rich talking to the minister. I stood by Brooke's side for a few minutes as she greeted her father, my daughter, and a few of the other bridesmaids. Just as I was about to excuse myself to go check my makeup, the most gorgeous man I'd ever seen walked into the room.

He was wearing a royal blue button-down with matching tie and a pair of gray slacks. Covering his dark eyes were a pair of wire-rimmed glasses. Hello, Clark Kent—would you like to be my Superman?

Before I had a chance to ask Brooke if she'd seen the hottie, she was stepping up onto her tiptoes to hug Clark Kent himself. Of course she'd seen him—she knew him. It was her wedding rehearsal after all. I scooted in closer in hopes of eavesdropping on their conversation. I wondered if Mystery Man was single? I wasn't originally planning on hooking up at my best friend's wedding, but it looked like plans may have changed.

"Blake, I'm so glad you could make it!" she said, giving him a peck on the cheek.

Wait–did she just say Blake? As in Rich's best friend, Blake? The best man, Blake? Yes, yes she did. Mission aborted. It was looking like I wouldn't be hooking up with Superman this weekend after all. Well, fuck me hard–or not.

The two continued having a much-too-private conversation while I stood awkwardly at Brooke's side. Hoping to gain her attention, I cleared my throat.

"Ahem."

"Oh, sorry, Cass. Blake, this is my best friend, Cassidy Carpenter. Cass, this is Rich's best friend, Blake Mitchell, or Early as these two knuckleheads call each other," she said, pointing toward Rich as he started walking toward us with the minister following closely.

Blake took my hand in his, and although it was an innocent shake it seemed like something more. I immediately began to wonder if he could feel it too. Who am I kidding? Of course he couldn't feel it. I'd officially lost my damn mind.

"It's a pleasure to meet you, Cassidy Carpenter," Blake said. Dear god, even his husky voice screamed sex on a stick.

"You too," I managed to croak out.

Just then, Rich joined our intimate little gathering. I'd never been so happy to see him as I was in that moment.

"Everything OK in there?" Brooke asked as Rich approached.

"Yep, I just wanted to go over a few things with the minister. We're ready to get this show on the road as soon as you're ready, Sweets," Rich said, pulling Brooke in for a tender kiss.

"Seriously, you two aren't even married yet," Blake chortled.

I smiled, wanting to get in on the jabs myself. "Do you two ever take a break? Get a room."

Blake turned toward me. "I like the way you think, Miss Carpenter," he said with a wink.

His words made me blush. I never blush. What the actual fuck was happening to me? "Thank you," I managed to stutter.

I put my head in my palm, and took a deep breath. I couldn't let on that this man was affecting me. Brooke would never let me hear the end of it. She turned back in my direction, and gave me a knowing look. I shrugged her off, hoping she would move on and forget about it. Luckily, before she had a chance to get me alone, the minister motioned for us to begin with the rehearsal.

"YOU LOOK LIKE you could use a cup of Joe," Rich whispered as he answered the door.

"Gee, thanks. I think that's code for . . . Wow, Cass, you really look like shit."

"You don't look like shit. You just look tired, that's all. Didn't you sleep well?"

"Something like that," I said, not wanting to tell Rich that I'd been tossing and turning for half the night thinking about his best friend. After several hours and a go-round with my vibrator, I'd finally succumbed to sleep—but, even then, Blake Mitchell had earned the starring role in my dreams.

"OK, clearly this is a conversation you'd prefer to have with my bride . . . So, if you could just give her this little gift from me then I'll be on my way. I want to get out of here before she wakes up—all that bad luck and all. Oh, and help yourself to some coffee because you really do look like shit," he said with a smirk.

"Fuck you," I said, picking up one of his shoes and throwing it in his direction. "You're such an asshole!"

"Be careful. Brooke will kill you if you give me a black eye on our wedding day," he joked.

"You better get out of here then!" I said, chucking the other shoe at him.

After spending much of the morning primping Brooke while also trying to avoid Blake, it was finally time to come face to face once again. I'd even tried to convince Brooke to change the ceremony structure and just have Blake stand up at the altar with Rich as I proceeded down the aisle by myself.

"Why would I do that?" she asked. "Let's just do it the way we rehearsed it last night. Unless there's really something else going on with you, and you're just not telling me," she added, eyeing me suspiciously.

"No!" I nearly shouted. "There's nothing going on. I just didn't want Rich to get cold feet up there alone and run, that's all."

"What would give you that idea?" she asked, panic rising in her voice. "Did he tell you something when you saw him earlier?"

I sighed, why did I even say something so stupid. A wedding planner like myself should know better. It's practically in our code of ethics not to get the bride upset seconds before walking down the aisle.

"No, Rich didn't say anything like that. He wants nothing more than for you to be his wife. Forget I even said anything. It was a silly suggestion, anyways. Now, let's go get you married," I said, pulling her in for a hug.

Brooke's dad, David, took his spot next to his daughter. I let them have a moment together before whispering in Kaity's ear. "You look beautiful, Baby Girl. Are you ready to walk your flowers up to Uncle Rich?"

She smiled up at me. "I got this, Mommy! I'm almost five."

"Yes, you're right. You're Mommy's big girl. Now when those

doors open, you start walking down the aisle, OK."

"OK," she beamed, her eyes locked on the giant cathedral doors. She was definitely a girl on a mission.

Before I even had a chance to step into my place in the processional line, I felt Blake's presence behind me.

Pausing, I took a deep breath before stepping back in line. Without even looking up to Blake, I linked my arm with his. Maybe I couldn't actually avoid him, but I could avoid these feelings I was having if I just didn't make eye contact.

"You look beautiful today, Cassidy," he said.

My pulse quickened at just the sound of his husky voice. Screw it, I had to see him. "Thank you," I said, looking up at him. He looked down at me, and a smile formed on his lips.

"I never thought I'd feel this again," he mumbled under his breath.

Before I had a chance to question what he'd said, the doors opened and the melody of Pachelbel's *Canon* filled the air.

I'D VOWED TO myself when Kaitlyn's sperm donor left me crumpled over and praying to the porcelain gods that I wouldn't allow any other man into my life–at least for anything more than a temporary fling. I built a wall that night–an unbreachable barrier around my heart that I needed to protect myself and most importantly to protect my unborn child.

I never expected one man to be able to weaken that wall with just a single look alone. I knew little about him, but I knew enough to know that I couldn't go there. I couldn't let this man shatter my bricks.

I hadn't met Blake Mitchell until last night, but Brooke had told me everything I needed to know. He was Rich's best friend– seriously, that should've been my first sign. Any friend of Dick

Davis shouldn't be a friend of mine. Ever since Rich came into Brooke's life, we'd always had this love/hate relationship. Truth is, I loved him like a brother, but if he ever hurt Brooke again, like he had last year after they lost their baby, then I would be charged with murder. He'd been warned, so I really considered it fair game.

All kidding aside, Blake was a widower. His wife, Alyssa, whom Brooke adored, was killed in a tragic accident. A drunk driver barreled into her car just weeks before Christmas. She was heading home from the toy store–the trunk of her car filled with packages. Luckily, their young daughter wasn't in the car that evening, and neither was Blake.

Alyssa was several months pregnant at the time with their second child, but managed to give birth to their premature son Benjamin before she succumbed to her injuries. According to Brooke, the pediatricians weren't sure if Ben would survive given his traumatic birth, but the little guy was a fighter. After just a month in the NICU, Blake was able to bring Ben home.

So, that was Blake Mitchell–a thirty-three-year-old widower, and single father of two. He had enough of his own baggage. He definitely didn't need to be further weighted down with mine.

I convinced myself that I was in an overly loving mood. My best friend was finally marrying the love of her life and, for a moment, I thought I wanted that, too. But, I didn't.

I'm a wedding planner. I see brides marrying their best friends all the time. Why should today be any different? Why should this best man staring back at me be any different than the hundreds of groomsmen I've come into contact with over the years?

I have Kaity and she's my world. I don't need a man to complete me. So, why am I standing here at my best friend's side with only eyes for the best man? The best man who has suffered so much loss in the past year. The last thing he needs, or wants, in his life is a relationship—especially a complicated relationship with this hot mess express.

I doubt he's even noticed me over here pining after him like a lost puppy. But Blake Mitchell makes himself difficult to not notice. For starters, he's huge. Brooke was right when she described the man as a tree. He's several inches taller than Rich who I've never thought was a short man. His shoulders nicely fill out the sports coat that he's wearing, and the day-old stubble outlining his chin sent a shiver down my spine. He'd replaced his glasses with a pair of contacts which only enhanced his chocolate-colored eyes. Just as I was taking in the rest of him, I noticed his lips curl into a small smile. Shit, I'd been caught–he'd noticed me after all.

Just as I'd decided to smile back–playing a game of cat and mouse as our two best friends said their "I do's"–I noticed a glimmer of light dancing across the wall. Following the reflection, I saw it came from Blake's ring finger–his wedding ring. The same ring that Alyssa had given him as they both vowed their unending love. If that wasn't the universe reminding me that I couldn't be interested in this man.

The sound of Brooke clearing her throat brought me back to the here and now.

"Earth to Cassidy," she said. "Can I have the ring? I'd like to get it on my husband's finger."

"Sure, it's right here," I said, holding out my thumb where I'd placed Rich's tungsten band.

"Thank you. And, don't think I won't ask about whatever is going on with you later," she whispered before turning back to her groom.

I sighed knowing that she would never let this go, but she had to let this one go—we both did. Besides, it was nothing–absolutely nothing. Thank you, Universe, for the subtle reminder.

Chapter Two

BLAKE

*I*T'D BEEN NINE days since I'd met Cassidy at Rich and Brooke's wedding, yet I couldn't stop thinking about her. Lord knows I've tried. I felt guilty–an undeniable heaviness in my chest. My head knew I wasn't cheating on my wife, but my heart felt otherwise. Another woman hadn't even sparked my interest since Alyssa's death. Truth be told, I hadn't even looked at another woman since the day I met her.

Rich had been on my back for the last few weeks about getting out more, but I didn't see a point. I knew he didn't want me to forget Alyssa, but he was worried about me. I understood; I just didn't care.

For the last ten months, I'd been walking around as if in a dense fog. The first month after Alyssa's death was all such a blur. After her funeral, I'd taken a leave of absence from my position with the *Times*. My only focus was on Ben and getting him well enough to come home. After spending a little over a month in the hospital, I was finally able to bring my baby boy home to meet his big sister. It should've been one of the happiest days of my life–instead it was filled with such sadness because their mother wasn't with us.

Every day since then, I've questioned how I'm going to do this alone. I've told myself repeatedly that I'll make it through–because as hard as it sounds to do it alone, the thought of doing it with someone other than Alyssa had been unbearable–until I saw Cassidy. And, for the first time in nearly a year, the heaviness had subsided.

For over a week, I'd been replaying the brief time we'd spent together. As much as she tried acting like she wasn't interested in seeing me again, I could tell I'd had the same effect on her as she had on me.

I'd been a groomsman in several weddings, and I'd never looked forward to the usually awkward bridal party dance–until now. I held Cass tighter than I probably should have as we swayed back and forth to "My Wish" by Rascal Flatts. I had to give Brooke credit, at least she'd chosen something slow instead of a party song where I wouldn't have been able to get my hands on her best friend. I'm a man. I think with my dick–I can't help it.

We danced in awkward silence with the rest of the bridal party for a few minutes before I finally worked up the nerve to tell her how I was feeling. The song was nearing the end and I knew it was now or never.

"I'd like to see you again before I head back to New York," I whispered in her ear, so only she could hear.

"Well you certainly don't waste any time, do you?"

"If I've learned anything over the last ten months, it's that you never know how much time you have. So why waste it?"

"You're right. I'm sorry," she said, shaking her head,

"Don't be sorry. Just say you'll see me again," I asked for a second time.

"I don't think that's a very good idea," she said, staring up at me.

"Why not? I saw you staring at me during the entire ceremony. You can't deny this chemistry between us."

"I can't," she said, pausing. "But that still doesn't mean it's a good

idea. Brooke has told me what you've been through, Blake. I'm not in any position to fix you. I can hardly fix myself."

"I don't need anyone to fix me. I just need someone to make me feel, and I can't explain what's happening, but I've felt more since I met you yesterday than I have in almost a year."

I could tell she was fighting with herself. Her body was saying yes, leaning closer into my chest, but her head was saying no. "I just–I just can't. I'm sorry. I'm not the right person for you. I wish I was, but I'm not."

Before I had another chance to convince Cass otherwise, the song ended, and Brooke motioned for her. I didn't see Cass again for the rest of the night. I'd assumed she snuck out after Brooke and Rich left the reception to take off to their tropical paradise.

The newlyweds had just returned from their honeymoon, and I'd stopped by their place to bring them sushi for dinner–a welcome home gift, of sorts. Truthfully, I just hoped I'd run into Cass. After all, she hadn't seen her best friend in nearly two weeks. I didn't think women could usually go that long without a little "girl time."

After the wedding, I'd made the last-minute decision to stay in Michigan for a few weeks. The kids loved spending time with Rich's niece and nephew so it seemed like a pretty reasonable thing to do. I'd also offered to stay and check on the house and collect their mail while they were in Fiji. I think Rich believed my reasoning, but I wasn't so sure that I'd convinced Brooke.

She was right in questioning my motives. I really cared more about spending some time with her best friend than the safety of their mail. Problem was, after Cassidy turned me down, I hadn't been able to get her cell number. And, although I'd tried running into her several times throughout my stay, I'd been unsuccessful. I was hoping that today would be my lucky day.

Knocking on the door, I waited a few seconds on the porch

before Rich answered. I eyed him suspiciously as he began buttoning his shirt.

"Seriously, Hot? You two were gone for two weeks–presumably fucking like rabbits–and you couldn't keep your hands off her for one evening?" I asked.

He glared at me before answering, "You could've called first. I texted you this morning, so I know your cell is working."

"I suppose I could've, but knowing that you have a monster case of blue balls is much more entertaining," I said with a smirk.

"You're such an asshole," he snarled.

"Is that a way to greet your best friend who just wanted to welcome you and your wife home? After all, I got your mail and, look, I even brought you some sushi for dinner. I figured you wouldn't have much food in the house after being gone for so long."

He looked down at the covered tray of Japanese cuisine I was carrying, noticing it for the first time. "Actually, I suppose that was nice of you. You can leave it, along with the mail, on the counter and get the hell out now," he said, patting me on the shoulder. "I'll call you tomorrow. We can catch up then. Maybe a round of golf?"

"A whole round," I asked, sarcasm evident in my tone. "You can actually go for four hours without getting laid?"

"Yeah, you're probably right. Maybe we should just shoot for the back nine," he joked.

Just as I was about to give into Rich's demands and get out of his house, Brooke called out from the bedroom.

"Rich, who was at the door?"

"It's just Blake. He was just bringing us some sushi for dinner. He's on his way out now!"

"Oh, that's so sweet," she yelled. "I'll be right out. Blake, you should stay and eat with us. I need to hear all about those babies.

I've missed them so much!"

I threw my head back in laughter, "Well, anything for you, Brooke! I'd love to stay."

Rich let out an audible sigh. "Well, since I'm not getting laid tonight, how about a beer? I think we still have some of those in the fridge."

"Sounds good, Man. I could use a cold one," I said, following him into the kitchen.

As Rich was leaning into the refrigerator, I noticed Brooke's phone sitting on the counter. Since Cass wasn't at their place, it was time to put Plan B into motion.

I reached for the phone only to find the fucking thing was passcode-protected. It was like the world was telling me to give up on this girl–good thing I'd always been up for a challenge.

"Hot, what's Brooke's passcode for her phone?"

"Why do you have my wife's phone?" he questioned, turning toward me.

This was going to be good. "Clearly so I can put a picture of my dick as her wallpaper," I deadpanned.

Instantly, I witnessed his rage brew from within. His jaw ticked and his face reddened. I could no longer stifle the laughter I'd tried to contain. "Relax, Hot. I'm just giving you a hard time. Give me a little credit. I'd like to think I'm a little more mature than that," I said, still laughing at his caveman antics.

"Oh," he said with a roll of his eyes. "I just figured you were trying to pay me back for all those stunts I pulled when you first started dating Lys."

I momentarily stilled at the mention of her name.

"Sorry, Man. I didn't mean to stir up those memories," he said, apologetically.

"Don't even worry about it. It's fine," I said, trying to reassure him. And, for the first time, it wasn't a lie. I really did feel fine. In fact, instead of the sorrow plaguing me for the last several months, I'd found hope. I wasn't exactly sure why, but I suspected it had something to do with a feisty blonde.

"Seriously, though, can I get Brooke's code? And, don't worry, it's not for a dick pic. I wouldn't want her to see what she's missing out on," I laughed, ducking to avoid the newspaper he'd just flung at me. "You're too easy today. Clearly, you're off your game. I just want to enter my mom's number in here in case she ever needs it in an emergency–you know, if she has the kids and needs it."

"Oh, sure," he said, shaking his head. "It's our anniversary–10/19."

"Isn't that sweet," I said with a phony gag.

"Whatever, fucker," he said, flipping me the bird.

Once I was finally in the phone, I scrolled through Brooke's contacts and quickly took a screenshot of Cassidy's information. I sent myself a text before deleting the evidence from the phone. Then I entered my mom's contact information–partly to cover my tracks in case Rich ever asked Brooke about it, and partly because it really was just a smart idea.

Just as I was sliding Brooke's phone back onto the counter, she entered the room and immediately coiled herself around her husband. He pulled her in for a kiss and the two began making out in front of me like two love-struck teenagers.

Rolling my eyes, I cleared my throat in hopes of subtly reminding them they weren't alone. Now that I'd accomplished my mission there really wasn't any reason to stay. If I wanted to keep my friend, I should probably let him relieve his problem down below. "Well, I think that's my cue to leave. I'll let you two newlyweds get back to it," I chuckled, turning toward the door.

"Don't leave on our account. We don't mind putting on a show. We could probably teach you a thing or two. Right, Sweets?" he said, looking down at a now mortified Brooke.

"Oh my god! No," she squeaked in embarrassment.

"Don't pay any attention to him, Brooke! I never have," I said, turning to exit.

I slid into my car and immediately opened the text message that I'd sent to myself from Brooke's phone. Pondering for a moment about whether to call or text Cass, I finally settled on calling her as it seemed like a more personal approach. It'd been years since I'd asked anyone out on a date, and I was starting to feel like I stunk at it.

I punched in her numbers, and waited for a moment before finally hitting send. Waiting for what seemed like eternity, Cass finally picked up the call.

"No, I'm not interested in buying your cutlery, consolidating my loans, or hearing about the terms of the exotic vacation I've supposedly just won. Please take this number off your call log, and don't ever call me again!" she shouted through the line.

"Cassidy, it's Blake Mit . . ." Before I had a chance to tell her my full name, she continued with her tirade.

"I don't care what your name is, asshole. I'm not interested in sending five thousand dollars to an offshore bank account." Before I could even get another word in, I heard a click. She'd hung up. It was on to plan—what was it now—Plan C? So much for the more intimate approach—I guess I'd have to send her a text message. Here's to hoping she even opens it.

> Blake: *Hey Cass, it's Blake Mitchell—Rich's best friend. We met last week at the wedding. But, you probably knew that . . . I just tried calling, but you thought I was a telemarketer. Anyways, I'm still in Michigan for just a few more days, and I was hoping you'd reconsider and have dinner with me?*

Hitting send, I waited for a few minutes hoping she would respond. Several minutes passed, and my text went unanswered.

Just as I was about to give up, the phone dinged beside me.

> *Cassidy: Hi, Blake. I'm sorry that I hung up on you. How'd you get my number?*

She didn't refuse my dinner date, but she didn't accept it either. In order to not sound like I was waiting for her response, I decided to head back to the hotel. Once I'd made the ten-minute drive back to the Holiday Inn, I quickly typed out a response.

> *Blake: I'm an investigative reporter. I've been able to dig up much more difficult numbers than yours. ;) I noticed you didn't refuse my request for dinner. Does that mean you've changed your mind?*

Immediately, I noticed the three little dots dance across my screen. I smiled, knowing she'd been waiting for my reply.

> *Cass: Brooke caved and gave it to you, huh? I didn't even realize they were home yet. Looks like I'm going to have some explaining to do.*

> *Blake: Still avoiding my question, I see. And, no, Brooke didn't willingly give me your number. Neither one of them know anything so you won't have to do any explaining. We'll just keep our dinner between us for now if you'd like. What time should I pick you up?*

> *Cass: I'm sorry, Blake. I haven't changed my mind. My answer is still no. It was great meeting you last week, and I hope you and your kids have a safe flight back to New York. G'night.*

Reading her response, I let out an audible sigh. This girl was frustrating. She was definitely playing hard to get. Good thing I like a good challenge. Game on, Miss Carpenter–game on.

Chapter Three

CASSIDY

*I*T'D BEEN OVER a month since I'd heard from Blake. I know I'd turned him down after he'd asked me out twice, but I guess I was hoping he would've tried harder. When he'd texted me, I'd so desperately wanted to accept his invitation, but I knew it just wasn't right. Even if we were to give dating a try–it just wouldn't work. We'd have so many obstacles to overcome–three children, a deceased wife, and my irrational fear of commitment. Not to mention, the nearly five-hundred miles between us.

Blake may not understand why I turned him down, but I was protecting myself. I'd let someone in before, and he'd left me broken. I just wouldn't allow it to happen again.

Since I was a little girl, I'd always loved fairy tales–especially the happily-ever-afters when Prince Charming married his princess and swept her off her feet to ride off into the sunset. It was probably why I'd made my career in the wedding industry. I just loved creating the perfect fantasy for my brides.

I'd always been known as the fun, witty, sassy, and sarcastic girl throughout high school and college, but I was also the hopeless romantic. I wanted nothing more than to be swept off my feet.

And, that's exactly what Steve Jackson did. He was a few years older, handsome and suave. We'd only dated for a short time, but I'd fallen and fallen hard. Everyone warned me to slow down–even Brooke had her reservations. She'd told me he seemed demanding, but I suppose I'd been blinded by love.

I'd been staring at the clock for the last forty-five minutes waiting for my last client of the day to decide on white or pink roses. After going back and forth for what seemed like forever, she finally picked yellow carnations. It was nearing eight o'clock and I needed to get to the pharmacy before closing. I was a week late, and even coffee wasn't enough to keep me awake these last few days. I was 99.9 percent certain I was pregnant.

After taking the test, the two pink lines confirmed my suspicions. I was nervous yet excited all at the same time. I knew it wasn't ideal because Steve and I had only been dating for two months, and we hadn't discussed marriage yet, but I knew he wanted a future with me. I couldn't have been more wrong.I called Steve right away, hoping to tell him my news over dinner. I was feeling too nauseous to cook, so I'd ordered Chinese food and had it delivered. The smell of the egg rolls alone sent me running to the bathroom which is where Steve found me–not the ideal fairy tale.

"What are you doing on the bathroom floor?" he questioned.

"What does it look like I'm doing?" I asked, resting my head in my palms.

"Well, I hope you're not contagious. I wish you would've told me you were sick. I definitely would've postponed dinner," he grumbled. "The sex isn't going to be any good if you're weak and lethargic."

Looking up at him, I could hardly believe the words coming out of his mouth–especially given my current state. I'd never heard him act so crassly before. He wasn't the most romantic, or chivalrous but I just assumed my expectations had always been too high.

"Don't worry, I'm not contagious," I said, wiping my mouth with

the back of my hand. "But, it's good to know that you only come over for the sex, though." I may have felt like shit, but I wasn't going to let him talk to me like that.

"Oh, you're feeling better then? And, you know I love that sassy mouth of yours–especially when it's wrapped tightly around my cock. Why don't we get you cleaned up and in the shower," he said, beginning to unzip his pants. Don't get me wrong, I did envision some pretty amazing sex tonight, but I wanted it to be in celebration.

"Steve! Stop for a minute, there's something I need to tell you," I said. After pausing for a moment, I blurted out the news, "I'm pregnant."

"You're what?" he questioned, his eyes darkening.

"Pregnant," I said, a bit louder this time.

"You slut! Who's the father?"

His words stung. How dare he call me a slut! I hadn't been with anyone else since we met.

"Why are you acting this way? You're the father! There's no one else," I screamed.

"I don't believe you! We haven't been together that long, and look at you," he sneered, his eyes traveling down my body, stopping at my belly. "You're already fat."

I just stared at him. My mouth agape. "Get out," I yelled. "Get the fuck out of here!"

"Well that's easy enough," he said. "Oh, and Cassidy, don't come after me later. Keep it if you want, but I don't want anything to do with you or your kid."

A few seconds later, I heard the door to the apartment slam shut. Steve had officially walked out of my life causing me to forget all about Prince Charmings and happily-ever-afters. I was certain those two things would never exist for me.

KNOCKING ON BROOKE'S door, I waited a few minutes before

letting myself in. I'd dropped Kaity off at her grandparents' house on the way over. I was in desperate need of some alone time with my best friend.

"Brooke!" I shouted, before noticing the distinct smell of smoke coming from the kitchen. The pungent odor was soon followed by the loud scream of the smoke detector. "Brooke," I yelled again, walking toward the kitchen to investigate. "Are you OK in there?"

"Yes, everything is fine," she yelled, as the beeping stopped. "I guess I'm just as terrible a baker as I am a cook. I tried making Christmas cookies, but it looks like I'll be buying them again this year," she added, holding up the burnt dough, which actually resembled hockey pucks more than cookies.

"You should've called. You know I would've come over to help. I love baking Christmas cookies!" I said, walking into the kitchen to find flour spilled all over the floor. "Dear lord, you really do need some help."

"Something like that," she laughed. "Grab an apron."

Pulling a black apron off a hook, I quickly slipped it over my head without looking at the front. Looking down, I tried making out the words. "I turn grills on," I slowly read.

I heard Brooke laughing behind me. "I bought that for Rich for his birthday. I think I found it funnier than he did."

"I think after all these years, I'm finally rubbing off on you," I chuckled. "This really is some funny shit. I'll totally wear it if he doesn't."

"I'm pretty sure he said the same exact thing," she said. "Now, are you going to help me with these cookies, or what?"

We'd just put the last two dozen cookies in the oven, and were working on cleaning the kitchen when Brooke asked me about Blake.

"Have you heard from Blake?" she questioned.

"How long have you been wanting to ask me about him?" I said, avoiding her question.

"Why? Did you think I'd forgotten?"

"I was hoping," I sighed.

"I know what you're doing. I'm not going to let you continue avoiding this topic. I know there was something going on between you two at our wedding," she said. "Now spill it."

"Nothing happened. I mean, yeah, I thought he was attractive. After all, I do have a vagina," I joked.

"Seriously. Can you not be Cass for like five minutes, and have a real conversation with me?"

"Sure, let me not be me. What the fuck does that even mean? I think I should just go," I yelled.

"I'm sorry," she said. "You know I didn't mean anything by it. I love you. But, sometimes when I want to have a serious talk, you put up a wall and joke about everything. I just worry about you, that's all."

"You don't have to worry about me. He did ask me out," I said. Brooke's eyes growing with my confession. "But, I turned him down. He doesn't need me in his life, and I don't need him, or any man for that matter."

"He's a good guy, Cass."

"Exactly. I'd just hurt him. And, he's already suffered a lifetime of hurt. So, just drop it, OK?" Before she had a chance to continue any further with our conversation, the oven went off.

"Saved by the bell," I said.

"For now," she sighed. "But, just so you know, Rich invited Blake and the kids to spend the holidays with us here in Michigan."

My pulse quickened with the realization that I might be forced to spend more time with him. I wasn't sure if I'd be able to control myself around him for a second time. I didn't know how to respond so I just stared at Brooke, hoping that she'd answer the questions without me having to ask her. In true best-friend fashion, she didn't disappoint. "To our surprise, he accepted right away. I think I now know why that was," she said, eyeing me suspiciously. "They'll be here the day after tomorrow."

I'd been home for the last hour, replaying the conversation with Brooke in my head. Twirling my cell in my hands, I'd contemplated calling Blake to ask about his plans. For all I knew, he'd met someone in the last month. Maybe he'd forgotten all about me. Why did I even care? Before I had a chance to think any more, my phone dinged with an incoming text.

> *Blake: I'm assuming Brooke told you that I'd be in your neck of the woods for the next few days?*

> *Cass: She did.*

> *Blake: I see you're still playing hard to get.*

> *Cass: I'm not playing, Blake. It's just not a good idea.*

> *Blake: I still think you're trying to convince yourself of that, Miss Carpenter. Have dinner with me on Wednesday?*

He wanted to have dinner with me the day after tomorrow? I wanted to see him, but I didn't think I could handle such an intimate setting.

> *Cass: I don't think I'll be able to find a sitter on such short notice. How about we take the kids sledding next weekend instead?*

Some people might think I was acting prematurely by getting our children involved, but it seemed like the safest decision to me. Kaity will just think she has some new friends, and I won't have to be alone with Blake. Besides, we'll be dressed in snowsuits–there's nothing sexy about that.

> *Blake: Are you asking my kids and me on a play date?*

> *Cass: Um, yeah, I guess I am.*

> *Blake: Sounds good to me. I think Maddy and Ben would love that as much as I would. How about we pick you up at eleven?*

> *Cass: Sure, but will you have a car?*

> *Blake: I'll borrow one of Rich's. He just doesn't know it yet.*

> *Cass: I like the way you think, Mr. Mitchell. ;)*

> *Blake: I don't think that's all you like.*

He was flirting with me. And, if I was being honest with myself, I think I was liking it. I smiled, knowing that I'd be seeing Blake again in just a few days. I texted him goodbye before laying my head back and drifting off to sleep.

Chapter Four

CASSIDY

*I*N JUST FORTY-EIGHT hours, I'd managed to bite all my fingernails down to tiny, little stubs. It was a nervous habit, one which my mother had tried to break me of for years. I sighed, knowing I was in desperate need of a manicure.

I didn't know why I was so nervous over this "play date." I'd gone on plenty of dates in my lifetime. I wasn't sure why this one was any different. Maybe because unlike all the others in recent years, I didn't plan on hitting and quitting it. Truthfully, as much as my body wanted to hit it, I knew I couldn't do that either. No, Blake Mitchell and I were just friends. And, not the kind with benefits–even if I did want to take him for a ride.

Glancing at my watch, I could see I only had about an hour before Blake would be picking us up. Catching my reflection in the bedroom mirror, I knew I needed to change my outfit. A skimpy tank top and jeggings were not going to keep me warm enough during our sledding adventure. Besides, I'm pretty sure my curves had curves in those pants.

Rummaging through my closet, I pulled out all the necessities–granny panties (you could never be too safe), leggings, leg warmers, jeans, snow pants, sports bra, camisole, long sleeve

T-shirt, sweater, puffy vest, gloves, scarf, and fuzzy ear muffs. Hopefully that would be enough layers to keep Mr. Mitchell's hands off me. I was half-tempted to dig out the chastity belt that Daddy had bought me before I left for college. He thought it was so funny–little did he know that ship had sailed long before then. It's a secret I'll take with me to the grave.

With just about five minutes to spare, Kaity waltzed into my bedroom. I chuckled at her choice of wardrobe. She was quite the fashionista–like mother like daughter. She looked like a mismatched Punky Brewster ballerina with striped knee-high socks over hot pink leggings, leopard print leotard, and silver-sequined tutu. Even her hair was pulled back into lopsided pigtails.

"Baby, I don't think you're going to be warm enough in that outfit," I said. "Do you think you can put your snowsuit on?"

"But, Mommy," she pouted.

"No 'But Mommying' me," I said, shaking my head. "Come on, do what I asked, please. Our friends are going to be here soon to pick us up. You don't want to have to stay home by yourself while I go with them, do you?"

"You can't leave me here alone, Mommy. I'm too little. You could go to jail," she chastised me while shaking her finger in my direction. Seriously, where does she learn these things?

"You're right, I guess we'll both have to stay home then," I said with a shrug.

"Fine," she huffed. "I'll wear my snowsuit, but can I still wear my ballerina skirt over it?"

"Sure," I agreed, rolling my eyes. "Now, hurry up, please."

Just as Kaity scurried back to her bedroom, the doorbell rang. Checking myself once more in the mirror, I took a deep breath and headed out to answer the door.

As much as I'd tried, I wasn't prepared to see Blake again. Even dressed in multiple layers, his long sleeve shirt hugged his firm biceps, and his black sweatpants left little to the imagination. Perhaps I hadn't thought this through as well as I'd hoped. *Allowing my date to wear sweatpants was pretty much setting myself up for a raging case of blue bean for the entire afternoon. What? You've heard of blue balls? Women get it too. It's a thing. I'm experiencing it right now–trust me!*

"Phew, is it hot in here?" I blurted out, fanning my face with my hand.

"Well, you are dressed for the tundra while standing in the middle of your living room where your thermostat is set at seventy-five degrees," he joked, pointing toward the little white box on my wall. "Did you think we were sledding in the Arctic?"

"You can never be too prepared, I suppose," I said, shrugging my cotton-stuffed shoulders.

"Yes, I suppose you're correct. Although, I wouldn't be opposed to you losing a few of those layers," he said with a wink.

"Daddy," said a little voice, reminding us that we weren't alone.

I looked down and for the first time spotted a tiny, towheaded little lady wrapped around Blake's right leg. In his left hand, he gripped onto a covered baby carrier.

"Hi there," I said, reaching down to pat Maddy on the head. "You must be Maddy. I've heard so much about you."

She stared up at me, her big blue eyes beaming. "Can you say 'hi,' Maddy?" Blake asked his daughter.

"Hi," she whispered, waving at me.

"And, I assume this handsome fellow is your brother Ben?" I asked Maddy, as I pulled the cover off the car seat.

"Yes, Daddy said he did a stinky in the car," she giggled, plugging her nose.

Her giggles were infectious, as Blake and I both threw our heads back in laughter.

"Well, since my darling daughter broke the ice, I do believe

Ben and I need to use your bathroom before we can head out," Blake chuckled.

"Not a problem. It's right down the hall and to your left," I said, pointing toward the bathroom.

Before Blake made it two steps down the hallway, Kaity ran out of her bedroom, her tutu now hanging around her neck.

"Oh, hi," she beamed. "You must be Blake. My name is Kaitlyn. I'm almost five. I live at 134—"

"That's enough, Kaity. I don't think Blake needs an outline of your resume," I laughed.

"Mommy, what's a rez-uh-may?" she asked, trying to sound out each syllable.

"Never mind, Kaity," I said, shaking my head. Luckily, Blake caught on that I needed a little bit of help with this one.

"Hi there, Princess. I am Blake. Your mom and Aunt Brooke have told me so much about you."

"You should take your coat off," Kaity responded.

"I think Blake's fine, Baby. We're going to leave right after he changes the baby's diaper."

"Oh, well, I just thought maybe he wouldn't be so hot."

Blake and I stared at her in confusion, before she continued. "You told Aunt Brookie that Blake was hot. I just thought he wouldn't be so hot if he wasn't wearing a coat," she said, with a shrug.

"Oh my god," I whispered, before burying my now reddened face in my hands. "I can't believe she just said that."

He turned back to me and whispered in my ear. "It's OK, Cass. I think you're pretty hot, too."

Blake loaded up the back of the SUV with the sleds I'd dug out of the basement. I'd even come across a tiny toboggan that Brooke had bought for Kaity when she was just about Ben's age. We'd just strapped the kids into their car seats and were backing down the driveway when Kaity piped up from the back seat.

"Mommy, I think I need to go potty."

"Kaitlyn! Did I not ask you to go potty before you put on your snowsuit?"

"Yes, you did, but I didn't have to go then!"

"It was five minutes ago!" I yelled.

"Please, Mommy! I really need to tinkle."

I sighed, knowing that this was probably Blake's worst first date ever. At least I wouldn't have to worry about him wanting to see me again. Without even having to ask, Blake drove back up the driveway.

I looked at him with a small smile. "I'm sorry," I mouthed.

"Don't even worry about it. I kind of know how this whole parenting thing works."

I'D STAYED AT the bottom of the hill for most of the afternoon, pulling Ben back and forth on the baby toboggan. He giggled as wet snow flew up around him.

"Again!" Kaity shouted, as Blake and the two girls reached the bottom of the hill for what seemed like the hundredth time. I couldn't help but smile at the three of them. Kaity riding sandwiched between Blake and Maddy down the hill.

She'd never really had a father figure in her life. Her grandparents took her regularly and doted on her like crazy, but it just wasn't quite the same. As much as I wanted that for her, I didn't want to open her up to inevitable heartache either.

"Kaity, why don't you let Blake rest for a while. He might be getting tired."

I knew that this type of activity was probably just a warmup for Blake's typical workouts, but I just wanted the excuse to be able to spend some time with him.

"I have a better idea," Blake said, grabbing the sled before hiking back up the hill. "Why don't you bring Ben up here, and I'll take the two of you for a ride. The girls can come down next to us."

"Yay! Please, Mommy," Kaity screamed, running back up the hill beside Blake.

"I think I like staying put at the bottom," I said, staring up the high hill.

"Miss Carpenter, are you afraid of heights?" Blake questioned.

"No, I just prefer staying close to the ground. That's all," I answered, quickly.

"Come on, you'll be fine," he said, making his way back down the hill.

"It's really fine. I enjoy watching you guys," I insisted.

"You're missing out on all the fun. Give me the baby," he said, reaching for Ben. "Now give me your hand."

He took my hand in his. As our skin touched, a shock of electricity zapped us.

"Oww," I giggled, yanking my hand back.

"My body can't help it. You're electrifying," he said with a smile.

"Oh my god. I think you've been friends with Dick for too long," I said, rolling my eyes.

"What are you talking about? Hot learned all his moves from me," he beamed.

"I think you both need a new instructor then," I laughed. "And, why the actual f-u-c-k do you call him Hot? You know that's done nothing but give Dick Davis an even bigger ego than necessary."

"Did you actually just spell f-u-c-k?" he chuckled, shaking his head.

"Um, yeah, we have innocent children listening to our every word. Kaity is already enough like me. She doesn't need to add cursing like a sailor to her list of attributes. Seriously, though, why Hot?" I asked again.

"I've been calling him that for years. It's actually the opposite of hot anyways. I'm really telling him that he's an ugly bastard. And, You'll have to forgive me for my awful pickup line. I guess it's been a while since I tried flirting with a woman who I like," he added. Suddenly our playful banter had taken on a more serious tone.

"Hopefully these will protect me from you." I said, shoving my hands back into my gloves. I took a deep breath, knowing that I'd need more than a thin pair of wool gloves to protect my heart from Blake Mitchell.

"You don't need to protect yourself from me," he said, locking his eyes on mine. "Now let's climb this hill–together."

I knew he was talking about the actual hill in front of us, but I couldn't help but think that he was speaking metaphorically as well.

"OK," I agreed, giving him my hand once more. After having to stop once or twice to calm my nerves, we finally made it to the top of the hill.

"Are you ready, Mommy?" Kaity asked as she patted the sled next to the one she and Maddy were already sitting on.

"Yeah, Baby," I said, hesitantly.

"You sit first," Blake said, putting his foot on the sled so it wouldn't slip out from under me. "I promise you'll be fine."

After I sat, Blake handed me Ben before getting into position behind me. He wrapped his strong arms tightly around me, making sure the baby was secure. I felt safe in his arms–safer than I'd felt in a long time.

"You ready?" Blake asked, digging his feet into the snow.

"As I'll ever be," I screamed, as he first pushed the girls off beside us before sending our sled flying down the hill behind them. The wind whipped around my face as the girls' giggles echoed through the chilly air.

"I really had forgotten how much fun that was," I laughed as we reached the bottom of the hill. "Let's do it again!"

"OK, but you do realize we need to get you back up there first?" Blake reminded me, pointing toward the top of the hill.

"On second thought, maybe I'll just watch from below," I said.

"I had a feeling you were going to say that," he said, planting a sudden kiss on my cheek. "I'm sorry, I probably shouldn't have done that."

"It's–it's OK," I said, staring up at him. Was I hoping he'd kiss me on the lips this time? Before I could give it a second thought, Maddy began pulling on her father's leg.

"Daddy, I sweepy," Maddy said, her eyes beginning to close.

"Well, I guess maybe it's time to call it a day," I said, patting Maddy on the head.

"Could I convince you two to come and have dinner with us back at the hotel room?"

"Hotel room?" I questioned.

"Yeah, I know it's not the most romantic place for dinner, but I really should get the kids down for a nap and that's where we're staying."

"Oh, right. You could come back to our place," I suggested, before realizing what I was even suggesting. "We could grab a pizza? I'm freezing in these clothes, and that way the girls could play after Maddy wakes up from her nap. I think Kaity would really have fun."

"Do you always think like a mom?" he asked.

"Ninety-nine percent of the time, yes, I do," I chuckled. "I'm sorry to say though I don't have any dry clothes at my place for you."

"It's OK, I threw an extra pair of sweats in Ben's diaper bag along with a change of clothes for the kids," he said. "You know, just in case."

Another pair of sweats? Sweet, Jesus. Sorry, Bean, no relief for you!

I'D THROWN EVERYONE'S wet snow outfits into the dryer, and started a pot of coffee before going back into the living room. Blake had taken his kids into the guest bedroom so they could get some rest before dinner. I was hoping Kaity would take a nap, too, but I knew that was probably asking for a small miracle. Unlike her mother, she didn't believe in naps.

I'd considered escaping to my bedroom to find some momentary relief for my "situation," but I knew that double-clicking my mouse wasn't an option–at least for the time being. The last thing I needed was for Blake, or even worse one of the kids, to walk in on me as my legs were spread-eagled in the air. My crotch on display like a rack of lamb on a Vegas buffet. No, as much as I wanted to give my bullet a spin, I'd have to wait until my houseguests had left, and my daughter was fast asleep in her own bed.

I walked toward the guest bedroom looking for Blake, assuming it was taking longer to get the kids down in a strange environment. Popping my head into the bedroom, I was surprised to see both little ones were already sleeping, but Blake was nowhere to be seen. Assuming he'd gone into the bathroom, I started back down the hallway until the sound of laughter from Kaity's room stopped me.

Walking back down the hallway, I poked my head through the doorway. I wasn't much of a crier, but the sight before me brought tears to my eyes. Blake was sitting cross-legged on the floor with Kaity beside him as the two were playing with her Barbie dolls. Smiling, I watched them for a few minutes in silence–my ovaries feeling as if they were exploding inside my body.

"You be Ken and I'll be Skipper," Kaity said, handing Blake one of her dolls.

"Why don't you want to be Barbie," he asked her. "I thought every little girl wanted to be Barbie."

"Mommy is always Barbie. She's beautiful just like her," Kaity said.

"Yes, your mommy is beautiful just like Barbie."

"Too bad I don't actually have an eighteen-inch waist," I muttered under my breath, not wanting to disturb them. I was just about to leave them to their playing when Kaity finally noticed me standing in the doorway.

"Hi, Mommy!" she said, as Blake glanced in my direction.

"Sorry, she cornered me as I was coming out of the other room. I thought it was difficult telling Maddy 'no,' but this one is very persuasive," he laughed.

"Yeah, tell me about it," I chuckled.

"Mommy, come play with us," Kaity said, patting the spot on the floor next to her. "I saved Barbie just for you."

"How about you watch one of your princess movies instead? Let Mommy and Blake have some grownup time."

"Please, Mommy. You and Blake should get married," she said.

As I nearly choked on my tongue, I felt my eyes simultaneously bug out of my head.

"What'd you just say?" I asked, thinking I clearly must have misunderstood her.

"You should be Barbie and you can marry Ken. She's already dressed in a wedding dress. See," she said, shoving the doll toward me.

Too stunned to argue, I sat down beside her, hoping Blake hadn't noticed my momentary freak out. If he had, he was gentleman enough to ignore it.

After several minutes of brushing Barbie's hair, and finding the perfect pair of heels for her wedding day, she was officially marrying Ken.

"Barbie and Ken should kiss," Kaity insisted. "They're married now."

"Baby, I think we've done enough playing. I'm sure we're boring Blake. We can play more later," I told her.

"But, you two should kiss, just like Ken and Barbie. You two like each other, right?" She said, innocently.

When had my daughter become such a little matchmaker?

"Kaity, where would you get that idea?" I asked, as Blake sat back with a smirk on his face.

"That's what people on your show do when they like each other. They kiss–a lot."

"Serves me right for thinking she wasn't paying attention when I watched my soap opera every day," I said, trying to explain the situation to Blake.

"That's TV, Baby. Remember how we talked about what TV is real and what is fake?"

"Yeah," she said, nodding.

"So, you don't kiss someone when you like them?" she asked.

"No, you can. It's hard to explain, I guess. I love you and I want to kiss you all the time," I said, smothering her in kisses.

"Mommy, you're silly!"

"You're silly, Silly Girl. Now let's put *Cinderella* on so Blake and I can talk and order dinner."

After setting up the movie, Blake and I went out into the kitchen to enjoy a moment of peace and quiet before the kids would join us for dinner.

I poured a couple cups of coffee as Blake took a seat on the couch. Setting his cup on the coffee table, I decided to sit in the chair instead of next to him on the sofa.

"So, care to tell me why you suggested going sledding when

you're afraid of heights?" Blake questioned.

Without fully explaining myself, I decided to go with a half-truth. "I just thought it was something that the kids might enjoy. I knew it would be difficult for us to both find sitters, especially since we didn't want to let Brooke and Rich know about our plans," I said. "Besides, I'm really not afraid of heights. I was just afraid I was going to slip down the hill, that's all."

"Oh, OK. If you insist. I suppose since you aren't afraid of heights then you'd be up for skydiving on our second date? Or maybe rock climbing? Oh, I know—tightrope walking?" he said with a wink.

I swallowed back the lump that had formed in my throat at just the mere mention of those suggestions. I wasn't entirely sure if it was the mention of the death-defying acts, or the talk of a second date that had me so worked up. "Um, sure," I said, hesitantly. They all sound like a lot of fun."

"Cassidy, relax. I'm only kidding," Blake said.

I chuckled. "I know."

"You're a terrible liar," he said, shaking his head. "But, it's OK because there will be a second date."

Chapter Five

BLAKE

AFTER THE BUSY day we'd had with Cass and Kaity, it wasn't difficult getting the kids to bed. Instead of watching some sports highlights before bed like I typically did, I decided to call it a night myself. But instead of falling asleep, I lay in bed staring up at the ceiling wondering what was happening between Cass and me.

It'd been a perfect afternoon–terrifyingly perfect. I'm man enough to admit, if only to myself, that I was scared shitless. I wasn't supposed to meet someone–at least not this soon.

I shut my eyes hoping sleep would come, but instead I tossed and turned all while envisioning Cass's perfect pink lips and how they would feel pressed against mine. I should've kissed her as we stood outside on her porch saying our goodbyes. Her eyes told me that she wanted it as much as I did, but I hesitated. My head tells me I'm ready, but my heart just isn't quite there.

Twirling my wedding band around my finger, I wondered what Alyssa would do if she was in my situation. Would I want her to be happy with someone else? I knew the answer was yes, but at the same time my heart pinged with jealousy.

"Lys, I think I met someone, and I need to know that you're

OK with it. Just give me a sign," I whispered. "I need to know if I'm doing the right thing here. I guess we probably should have talked about this, but we thought we had our entire lives ahead of us. You were so young."

Before I had much more time to dwell on the fact that I was lying in a hotel room asking my deceased wife permission to kiss a girl, I heard Maddy cry out from her crib beside me.

"Right there, Baby," I said, slipping my feet out from underneath the covers.

Before I'd even rolled out of bed, her whimpers became full-blown sobs.

Flipping on the light, I saw Maddy standing in her crib, tears streaming down her reddened face.

"Daddy's here, Baby," I said, trying to soothe her. "Did you have a bad dream?"

"No," she cried, shaking her head. "I miss Mommy."

I swallowed back my own feelings before responding, "I know, Baby. I miss her too." Maddy was still so young. I wasn't even sure what she remembered about Alyssa. Her confession definitely caught me off guard. She hadn't mentioned Alyssa in months, and I didn't often bring her up. I'd decided that I would wait until Maddy was older, and would better understand what had happened rather than just further confusing her now.

I had a feeling spending the day with Cass and Kaity stirred up some of her memories. Listening to Kaity call Cass "Mom," must've triggered something inside her. Was this the sign that I'd asked Alyssa for? Maybe? But what did it even mean?

"I don't understand what you're trying to tell me here, Short Stack," I said under my breath.

"Daddy, can I sweep with you?" Maddy asked, wiping her damp cheek against my T-shirt.

"Sure, but don't wipe your snotty nose against me again, Silly

Girl," I laughed. "I think as a punishment, the tickle monster is going to get you," I added, tickling her sides.

"Daddy, Daddy! That tickles," she yelled between laughs.

Her laughter was infectious. Just like her mother's.

We both crawled into bed, my daughter snuggling into my side. That's the last thing I remember before sleep finally claimed us both.

"I should probably head home. I have a midterm in my corporate law course next week and I haven't even begun to study," Alyssa said as the movie she'd picked came to an end. Whom was I kidding? I didn't even know what the movie was about or who starred in it. We'd spent most of the last two hours cuddled together on the floor making out like horny teenagers.

"Anything I can say to change your mind?" I asked, batting my eyes.

She giggled, "Why do you have to be so damn cute?"

"Cute? You just think I'm cute? Puppies are cute, Lys! I'm a man. I should be rugged and sexy!" I joked.

"You're right. You're so dreamy and hunky," she tittered.

"I'll get you for that!" I screamed, as I rolled on top of her, pinning her to the floor.

"Blake, get up! I really need to get going," she laughed. Her laughter only intensified as I grabbed her sides and began tickling her. "Oh my god. Stop! I'm going to pee my pants!" After a few torturous minutes, she squirmed her way on top of me. We both came to a halt when we realized the position we'd put ourselves in. We'd only been on a few dates, and although I was ready to take things to the next level, I didn't want to pressure Alyssa into anything.

"I'm sorry, Lys. I was just trying to have some fun. If I crossed the line, I apologize," I said, looking up into her eyes. I wanted her to see my sincerity—how much she really meant to me.

"It's OK, Blake. I know you were trying to behave. You may have failed, but I'll give you an A for effort," she winked. "And, as much as I

don't want to end this tonight, I really do need to get going."

"I understand. Can I see you again soon?" I asked.

"Of course. I'll call you after my exam, and we can meet up. Maybe we can finish what we started here tonight," she flirted.

This woman was going to be the death of me and I was only twenty-two years old. "Don't make any promises you can't keep, Alyssa," I growled.

"Don't worry, Blake. I don't," she sassed, as she got up and gathered her purse and coat. *"Next time."*

I woke up just as the sun began peeking through the curtains. I'd spent the entire night alternating between dreams of Alyssa and Cassidy. My mind was at war with my heart, and I was definitely in the middle of a losing battle.

Rolling over onto my side, I was startled to see my daughter awake and staring back at me.

"Morning, Baby Girl. Daddy didn't know you were already awake over there," I said, reaching over to grab Maddy's little pinky finger. "You were so quiet."

"I was letting you sweep, Dadda. You wooked tired."

"Thank you, Maddy. Daddy feels much better now. Are you hungry?"

"Yes, pancakes, please. With wots and wots of syrup."

"Well then, let's get your brother up, and we'll go get you an order of fluffy pancakes with extra syrup," I said, kissing her on the cheek.

I'D BUNDLED THE kids into their winter gear and stuffed them into the back seat of the SUV I'd borrowed from Rich. I probably should've called Cass this morning, but I wasn't sure what I'd say after my fitful night of sleep. After a short drive to the local diner, I was unloading the kids when I heard a familiar voice come up from behind.

"Well if it isn't Blake Mitchell," Brooke beamed. "I thought we would've heard from you yesterday. I only knew you'd made it to town because one of our cars was missing."

"Yeah, sorry about that. We were all a little tired and Ben wasn't feeling well so we decided to stay at the hotel for most of the day," I lied.

"Daddy, can we go swedding again?" Maddy interjected, pulling on the side of my leg.

Brooke eyed me suspiciously before turning to Maddy. "When did you go sledding, sweetheart?"

"Back in New York before we left," I shouted, not allowing Maddy a chance to answer.

"No, Daddy. We swedded here. Member?" Maddy insisted.

"Crazy kids. They say the darndest things," I laughed.

"Uh huh," Brooke said. "Whatever you say, Blake. What do you say you buy me breakfast? I'm meeting Cass and her daughter here in a few minutes."

I laughed under my breath, "We wouldn't want to intrude on girl time. We'll just get a booth in the corner. You won't even know we're here."

"Nonsense. Besides, I know you've been trying to reach Cass. This would be the perfect time," she winked.

"I don't know, Brooke. And, what would Rich say about you trying to play matchmaker?" I joked.

"What Rich doesn't know won't hurt him. Besides, you owe me breakfast for borrowing one of my cars."

"Fine, you win," I laughed. "Lead the way."

As we walked into the diner, I noticed Cass already sitting in a booth toward the rear of the restaurant. Her blond hair cascading over a bright red sweater. Sitting with her back to us, she seemed startled when I approached from behind.

"Fancy meeting you here, Miss Carpenter," I said, placing my hand on her shoulder.

"Blake," she said, nervously. "I wasn't expecting to see you here. I don't mean to be rude, but we're meeting Brooke here, and I still don't think it's appropriate for her to see us together."

"Too late for that, Cass. She already saw us in the parking lot. She's the one who invited us to eat with you guys," I said, pointing toward Brooke, who was making her way toward us.

"Wait, what?" Cass asked, sounding alarmed.

"Don't worry," I whispered. "I didn't tell her about yesterday. Our secret is still safe–for now."

"Hey, Cass!" Brooke said, bending over to place a peck on her friend's cheek. "I assume Blake told you that I invited them to eat breakfast with us?" she asked, scooting into the booth next to Cass and Kaity as I took the opposite side with Maddy and Ben.

"Yep, he sure did," Cass said, sarcasm evident in her voice.

"Hi Maddy! Hi Ben!" Kaity beamed.

"Kaity, you've met Maddy and Ben?" Brooke asked curiously.

Without giving Kaity a chance to respond, Cass interrupted her daughter, "Yeah, they met at the wedding."

I internally groaned at her admission knowing that my children weren't at Brooke and Rich's wedding. "Blake's kids weren't at my wedding," Brooke responded.

"What? Oh, what I meant was just that Kaity has seen pictures of them at your place. That's all."

"No, Mommy! I met them yesterday, remember!" Kaity piped up.

Biting down on her lip, Cass turned and glared at her daughter.

"You two saw each other yesterday?" Brooke questioned, suspiciously. "Blake, I thought you stayed back at the hotel all day because Ben wasn't feeling well?"

How was I going to get myself out of this one? "You're right.

You caught us. We ran into Cass and Kaity at the pharmacy that's all," I explained.

"Swedding Dadda, swedding!" Maddy yelled.

Shit! These kids were going to give us away. "Yes, Baby. We'll go sledding after breakfast," I said. "She's been begging to go sledding ever since we got here," I laughed, addressing Brooke.

"Uh huh," Brooke said, not seemingly convinced with our explanation. "I don't know what's going on here, but I suppose I'll let it go for now. Just know, I do know that you two are hiding something from me, and I'll figure it out later."

Finishing our breakfast, the kids and I left the girls alone for some chitchat–or whatever it is that women do when they're alone. Do their nails? Brush their hair? Talk about their upcoming visit to the pussy doctor? Who the fuck knows, really. It was an unfathomable mystery that men would never understand.

Before pulling out into traffic, I shot Cass a quick message to apologize for leaving her alone to suffer through Brooke's interrogation.

> *Blake: I'm sorry I left you alone. I hope she isn't being too hard on you.*

> *Cass: Yeah, you're an asshole, lol. Luckily Kaity had to use the bathroom so I was able to escape her for a few more minutes. I have no idea what to tell her. I feel horrible lying to my best friend and right in front of my daughter! I'm a horrible mother!*

> *Blake: You're not a horrible mother. Just don't be alarmed when your daughter turns into a lying, cheating kleptomaniac by the time she's sixteen and you get a call to bail her out of jail.*

> *Cass: Oh my god! Shit! I have to tell Brooke the truth. Fuck, Kaity*

already knows I lied. I've ruined my daughter. This really is all my fault!

Laughing, I realized Cass didn't understand that I was being facetious. I suppose that's the problem with text messages.

Blake: Cass, calm down. I was only kidding. Kaity won't end up being a kleptomaniac, I promise. I think it's best if you don't tell Brooke about our date yesterday. At least until we can talk.

Cass: You're an asshole.

Blake: You already said that. ;)

Cass: Well, it's true.

Blake: Well this asshole would like to see you again. We're leaving the day after Christmas. What do you say?

Cass: I need to get back out there, or Brooke will send a search party into the bathroom. I'll let you know.

Tossing the phone into the passenger seat, I smiled, knowing she hadn't turned me down flat this time. "We're making progress, Miss Carpenter," I said to myself, shifting the car into gear and pulling into traffic.

Chapter Six

BLAKE

A LIGHT SNOW began to fall as I turned down Cass's road. I sighed in relief when I saw her car in the driveway. Not having much time, I had to see her before leaving in the morning. We hadn't seen each other since our meeting at the diner a few days earlier. After the kids and I'd spent the last few days with Rich and Brooke celebrating the holiday, it was easier than I thought it'd be to sneak away for a while. Telling them that I needed to run out and grab some diapers before our trip back, they agreed to watch the kids while I ran to the store. Yep, I continued to lie to my best friend; I was a jackass.

Debating back and forth about giving her this gift–it really did seem too soon–I wanted to pursue whatever this feeling was between us, and I didn't see any other way. Grabbing the wrapped packages from my trunk, I made my way up to her doorstep. Before I'd even had a chance to knock, she'd opened the door.

"Hey, Blake, I didn't expect to see you," she said, surprise evident in her voice.

"No? Then why'd you answer the door before I'd even knocked?" I asked with a wink.

Scrunching her nose, she responded, "Because I saw you pull

into my driveway. I'd been watching the snow come down. I just heard an updated forecast on the news. They're saying we could get six inches now overnight."

"That's not the only thing that could give you six inches overnight," I said under my breath.

Pretending to ignore me, her reddened cheeks betrayed her. "Well are we going to stand here all night talking about the weather, or did you want to come in?" she asked.

"Yeah, I'd like that, but I can't actually stay for too long. Rich and Brooke think I ran to the store to grab some diapers. I wouldn't want them to get even more suspicious than they already are. Brooke must've asked me fifty questions today about us," I explained.

"Yeah, she's given me the third degree, too," she sighed.

"Maybe we should just tell them?" I asked, hoping she would agree.

"No! I still don't think that's a good idea. Besides, we just went out once, Blake. There's nothing going on to even tell them about," she said, shrugging her shoulders.

This girl was frustrating beyond belief. If only I could get her to open up and tell me why she was so hesitant, but if she insisted on waiting–I would wait.

"OK, if you insist," I said, stepping into the hallway as she closed the door behind me. "How was your Christmas?" I asked, trying to change the subject.

"It was nice. We just got home. Kaity and I spent the day with my parents," she explained. "Yours? I figured you'd be busy watching your kids play with all their Christmas gifts. I'm sure Brooke spoiled them rotten. She certainly bought my daughter too much this year," she added, her eyes darting as if I made her nervous.

"Yeah, she certainly did, but it was good for them. Last year . . . ," I paused before continuing, swallowing back the emotion in my voice. "Last year was really difficult on all of us. We'd lost Alyssa just a few weeks before Christmas so we didn't celebrate at all. I'm glad they could celebrate again this year with some sort of normalcy."

"I'm sorry, Blake. I didn't mean . . . ," she trailed off.

"It's fine. Don't even worry about it. Actually, I'm here because I have a gift of my own."

"Brooke sent you over here with another gift?"

"No, I hope I'm not being too forward, but I brought you a present."

She stared at me, her eyes widening, "Well it hasn't stopped you before. In fact, I'm

starting to think that 'forward' is really your middle name."

"You know you're adorable when you act angry," I said, placing the package in her hand. "Now don't argue with me. Just open it."

She looked down at the brightly wrapped box for a moment before untying the silver ribbon I'd knotted around the package.

"You really didn't have to get me anything. I feel bad because I don't have anything for you," she said, apologetically.

"It's fine, Cassidy. I wasn't expecting anything. I just really wanted to give you this. Now stop stalling and open it. That'll be gift enough for me."

Without saying another word, she ripped off the paper and opened the box, revealing two airline tickets.

"What are these?" she gasped.

"They're two plane tickets," I responded.

"I can see that, but why are you giving me plane tickets?"

"I want you and Kaity to come visit us in New York after the first of the year. I know you're going to argue with me that it's too soon, and you're probably right. But, the truth is, I'm leaving in the morning, and I can't imagine not seeing you again. I want you to see the city. See my home. See where I work. Who knows, maybe you can make some work contacts for yourself while you're there. I'm sure some of the people in my office have contacts with some of the top fashion designers in Manhattan. They'd have to know something about wedding dresses, right?" I asked, sounding hopeful.

"Blake," she said, interrupting me.

"Cass, please, just let me finish before turning me down," I interjected. Before I had a chance to finish my plea, Kaity came running out from her bedroom. She was dressed in bright red leggings and what could only be described as a tacky Christmas sweater–with a light-up reindeer nose and all.

"Mommy, can we watch a Christmas movie," Kaity asked without noticing me standing there.

"In a little bit, Baby, we have company right now."

Looking up, Kaity beamed when she noticed me standing there.

"Hi, Blake!" she said, wrapping her arms around my waist. I only wished that Kaity's mother had shown the same enthusiasm when I appeared at their door. "Are Maddy and Ben here," she asked, looking behind me.

"No, Princess. They're with their Uncle Rich and Aunt Brooke."

She turned to Cass before responding, "Do Maddy and Ben have the same Uncle Rich and Aunt Brooke as I do?" she questioned.

"Well, kinda," Cass began to answer. "You know what. Yeah, you do. I guess you're cousins."

"Oh OK," Kaity shrugged, accepting Cass's explanation. "Is that present for me?" she asked, noticing the package I was carrying.

"Kaitlyn! Don't be rude," Cass yelled.

"It's OK, Cass. It is actually for her," I said, handing the box over to Kaity.

"Thank you," she mumbled as she immediately ripped into the paper revealing a stuffed New York teddy bear. "Mommy! Look! It's just like the bear that Auntie Brooke gave me only littler! Now I have the mommy and the baby!"

I smiled knowing that I'd done well. Remembering that Rich had taken Brooke to NYC, I only assumed that she'd brought Kaity back a gift. It only seemed natural for her to pick out a stuffed toy–after all, what little girl didn't love the original Teddy Bear? Of course, she'd like a matching bear. It only helped my cause that Brooke got her the extra-large version.

"That's pretty sweet, Baby. What do you tell Blake?" Cass said, eyeing me suspiciously.

"Thank you, Blake," Kaity said, hugging me again.

"You're very welcome. But, I have more," I said, bending down to her level.

"You do?" she said, her eyes beaming.

"Yes, I do," I nodded. "How would you like to visit the toy store where your Aunt Brooke and I bought those bears?"

"Wow, really? I can do that? Can Mommy come, too?" she asked.

"I'd like that very much," I said, winking at Cass who was now giving me the death stare. "I think you should ask your mommy."

"Mommy, can we? Please can we visit the toy store?" Kaity begged.

"That's low, Mitchell. I can't believe you're using my daughter against me," she argued, pursing her lips together.

"Come on, Carpenter. You know you want to," I said, smirking.

"Fine, we'll come. But only because you're right about making the work contacts. It really could boost my business. Oh, and we're getting a hotel. We're not staying with you," she sassed, putting her hands on her hips.

"Whatever you say. I'll see you in a few weeks. And, by the way, that's a win for me," I retorted, leaning over to place a gentle kiss on her forehead.

"You're ridiculous," she said, rolling her eyes.

"I'm charming, and you like me," I chuckled.

"Whatever you say," she laughed, shrugging her shoulders.

As much as I enjoyed seeing this lighter side of Cass, I really did need to get back with the kids. "I should probably get going. We wouldn't want our friends getting any more suspicious."

"No, I guess you're right," she sighed, seemingly disappointed that I needed to leave. "Kaity, can you go back in your room and play while I say goodbye to Blake, please? Then we can watch your Christmas movie."

"OK, Mommy. Bye Blake!" she said, skipping down the hallway toward her bedroom.

"So, I guess I'll see you soon then," Cass said, staring up at me as she bit down on her bottom lip.

I couldn't hold back any longer. The way she looked at me–her eyes, an entrance to her soul and the way her chest fell with each shallow breath she took. She wanted this as much as I did. I needed to feel her lips against mine; I needed to taste her.

Without another thought, I pulled her against me, gently placing my lips on hers. Our kiss was slow at first, neither of us ready to play the aggressor. After several moments, I parted her lips with a flick of the tongue as our mouths began dancing together in a perfect harmony. Feeling her fingers slide through my hair, I nearly picked her up and carried her into the bedroom. As her chest pressed into mine, her heartbeat accelerating, it took everything within me to draw away from her.

I never thought I wanted to feel another woman's lips against mine. I never thought I needed another first kiss, but in that moment, as much as Alyssa was my past, Cassidy was my present. And, if I had it my way–she'd be my future. I'd never been one to run from love and, lord knows, I wasn't about to let her run from me.

"I really should go," I groaned, breaking away from her lips.

"OK," she whispered, touching her fingers to her mouth. "We'll see you in a few weeks then."

"You will, but we'll talk before then," I said, opening the door and stepping out onto the porch. "Oh, and Cass, you did give me the best gift that I could've wished for. Merry Christmas."

"Merry Christmas, Blake," she said, her cheeks beginning to redden from my admission.

Chapter Seven

CASSIDY

*T*HE PREVIOUS TWO weeks passed by in the blink of an eye. Spending New Year's Eve with Brooke and Rich, I had to sneak off to the restroom in order to Facetime Blake at midnight. We'd spent nearly every night since then on the phone, and I was actually looking forward to seeing him again.

Brooke, of course, continued to give me the third degree when I told her Kaity and I were visiting New York. I tried to convince her it was just a work trip, but she finally got me to admit that I'd also made plans to see Blake while we were in the city. Little did she know, the entire trip was actually his doing and on his dime. She'd even offered to watch Kaity while I was gone, but I insisted that it'd be a cultural experience for her. Convinced I'd return home to a bevy of questions, I was just thankful that she'd finally agreed to my terms–at least for the time being.

Glancing over my side, I watched momentarily as Kaity struggled to find her seatbelt.

"It's not like the car, Baby. It fastens at your lap–like this," I explained, reaching over her tiny legs to clasp the buckle, making sure to pull it extra tight.

I strapped myself in before listening to the flight attendants' emergency instructions. Did she say to exit at the front, or at the rear? I didn't fly much, and my nerves began to get the best of me. Wiping my sweaty palms against my jeans, I blew out a deep breath. I needed to relax, or Kaity would soon sense my fear, and I didn't want that. This was her first time flying, and so far she was a champ. Doing much better than her mom anyway.

Leaning my head back in the seat, my mind began to swirl over the hum of the engines.

I can't believe I was actually doing this. Letting a man sweep me off my feet and fly me, first-class no less, off on a getaway. I definitely didn't believe in love at first sight, or this insta-love bullshit, but here I was going goo-goo ga-ga over this man. I wasn't sure if my heightened nerves were because we'd soon be thirty-nine-thousand feet in the air, or because I was taking a chance with Blake. They were both risks that I wasn't used to taking–both equally as terrifying.

With a little help from the five tiny bottles of Prosecco the flight attendant had kindly given me, I wasn't feeling a thing as we began our descent. First class was definitely the way to travel. Blake had certainly ruined me for all future adventures. I wasn't sure if I should thank him or yell at him–after all, it's not like I had a ton of extra cash coming in this time of year. Most Michigan brides don't dream of winter weddings, at least after the holidays.

Turning toward Kaity, I saw she'd fallen asleep watching her Disney movies on the portable DVD player we'd brought along. Gently shaking her shoulder, she stirred in the reclining seat next to mine.

"Kaity, wake up," I whispered into her ear. "We're about to land, and you don't want to miss seeing the Statue of Liberty!"

"Is that the big lady we talked about? The one from . . . ?" she paused for a moment, trying to remember what we'd talked about.

"Yes, the one from France. Do you remember where France

is?" I asked, hiccupping from the aftermath of the bubbly.

Pondering my question, she scratched her chin before responding. "Is that in Texas?"

"No, France is a country in Europe. It's pretty far away. We'd have to cross that entire ocean to get there," I said, pointing down to the water below.

Her eyes got bigger as she looked down at the Atlantic. "Wow, it must take an entire year to get there! That water looks so big!"

I chuckled at her innocence, "Not quite a year, but probably an entire sleep. Look there she is–there's Lady Liberty."

"Wow, she looks old and shiny. Will we get to see her closer?"

"Probably not this time. It's still pretty cold outside. Besides, Blake might have other fun stuff planned for us," I explained as I felt the wheels hit the tarmac. "Get your stuff together so we can meet our friends."

TEXTING BLAKE THAT we'd landed, we headed toward the baggage claim area. I'd planned to get a taxi after we collected our items, but he'd once again surprised me and said that he already had a car outside ready to take us back to his place. This man was definitely swooning me, and as much as I hated to admit it, I was falling for it–and maybe even him.

A little unsteady from the Prosecco, we'd nearly made it to the baggage claim when I stumbled over my own feet. Preparing to fall, I was shocked when a pair of extra-large, masculine hands caught me from behind.

With my back to the mystery savior, he wrapped his arms around me, holding me steady with his hands resting just below my breasts. It may have been the Prosecco talking, but I felt safe wrapped in this stranger's embrace. Leaning back into him, he spoke before I even had a chance to turn around.

"Looks like I found you right on time," he said. I wasn't sure if it was the alcohol, or the husky timbre of his voice, but a chill rolled down my spine.

"Blake?" I whispered. "Is that you?"

"Were you expecting someone else," he growled.

"Well, yes, I didn't expect to see you here. I thought when you said there was a car here that someone else would be driving it. I'm glad it's you though," I said, leaning further into him. "Sounds like someone is jealous?"

Before standing me back on my feet, he placed a gentle kiss on my neck. "Maybe a little," he confessed, whispering in my ear. "But, I guess that'll have to do for now."

Looking at him with confusion on my face, he continued. "I've been waiting two weeks to kiss you."

"You're so smooth, Mitchell," I said, rolling my eyes.

"I must be doing something right. I have you literally falling for me," he said with a smirk.

"Haven't we talked about your cheesy pickup lines?" I laughed.

"Yeah, but since I was your knight in shining armor, I thought you'd forgive me."

"Yeah, you're probably right. And, where did Kaity go?" I asked, panic setting in. I shouldn't have drunk that much on the flight. That wasn't typical of me.

"She's right over there," he said, pointing toward the row of benches just a few feet from where we were standing. "She's been playing with her electronic game. I've been watching her the whole time."

Sighing in relief, "Looks like you're her knight in shining armor, too."

"I'll protect both of you–always. Now let's get going. I think you need a nap. How much did you actually drink on that flight?"

"More than I care to admit," I giggled, trying not to read too much into his comment about protecting us.

It was nearing sundown when we finally checked into the hotel. For the last two weeks, Blake kept insisting that we could stay in his spare bedroom, but I'd stuck to my guns. I'd told everyone that this was a business trip, and I knew if I stayed with Blake that someone would be sure to find out about our arrangement–whatever that may be. I kept trying to convince myself that we were just friends, but after that kiss a few weeks ago, I knew it was turning into something more.

"Are you sure I can't get you to change your mind? We can always tell the front desk clerk that we found a bedbug in the room, and they'd be forced to refund your money," he said, unlocking the room with a swipe of the keycard.

"Ewww! You better not have just jinxed me," I said, as I began itching my arm. "See, look what you've done! Now I'm itchy all over!"

"A shower might cure that," he said with a playful smile, wheeling my suitcases into the room.

"Oh, that's a great idea! I guess that's your cue to leave then."

"Oh, I thought we could take one together."

"Did you forget my daughter is staying in this room?" I asked, pointing toward Kaity who was still engrossed in her princess game.

"I'm sure my mom wouldn't mind taking her for the night. After all, she already has Maddy and Ben. Actually, she'd probably love the help!"

"I'm not sure your mother would consider an additional five-year-old as help," I laughed. "Besides, I have a major headache from all that Prosecco, and I'm exhausted from the flight. I think I might just start a new book and crawl into bed."

"You don't even want to get dinner?"

"I'm sorry. I'll probably just order a pizza for Kaity, or maybe some room service. I hope you didn't have anything fancy planned for tonight."

"Nah, not really," he said, sounding upset.

"You don't sound so sure about that."

"I didn't have anything specific planned, but I haven't been kid-free for nearly two years. I'm just not really sure what to do with myself. I was hoping I could spend the evening with you two. Maybe show you around the city?"

I felt bad leaving Blake alone for the evening after we'd just arrived, but I really didn't feel up to a night on the town either. "Do you just want to get dinner and eat here with us?" I asked, before thinking about my suggestion.

He studied my expression for a moment before answering, "Um, sure. If you're really fine with it then I'd like that a lot."

"OK, then. If you don't mind, I really do think I'd like to hop in the shower–alone. Would you mind ordering dinner for us?"

"No, I can do that. Do you or Kaity have any allergies, or preferences?"

"Spoken like a true dad," I laughed.

"Yeah, I guess so," he chuckled. "Seriously, though, do you?"

"No, we're both fine with whatever you'd like as long as you don't try to feed me fish eggs."

"One order of caviar coming right up," he joked.

"Very funny," I sassed, stripping my clothes before sashaying into the bathroom. Closing the door behind me, I leaned up against it and gazed at myself in the mirror, smiling at my boldness. The look on Blake's face as my clothes dropped to the floor was priceless. Even though I was still covered by a bra and boy shorts it wasn't something I'd typically do. The alcohol had really done a number on my senses.

Turning on the faucet, I removed my undergarments and stepped under the hot water. Deep down, I'd hoped that Blake would join me, but I knew he wouldn't do that with Kaity just in the other room. He talked a big game, but Blake Mitchell was nothing but a gentleman.

Closing my eyes, I leaned against the wall and imagined what Blake would do to me with those firm, strong hands of his. Those same hands which had rescued me from a near disaster just hours earlier. Squirting a dab of coconut-scented body wash into my palm, I began rubbing the soap across my breasts. Inhaling the fresh scent, I could easily envision the two of us rolling around on a sandy beach as the sun began to set in the distance.

I tweaked and pinched my nipples as water cascaded around me, pooling at my feet. Not being able to resist the tension that was building between my legs, I slid my left hand lower as my right hand continued to palm my breasts. Through the water clinging to my belly, I slipped my hand to my core and gently inserted one finger. Arching my back in pleasure, my elbow hit the bottle of body wash, knocking it off the shower shelf. Without bothering to pick it up, I added a second finger before using my other hand to rub my clit.

After just a few minutes of self-pleasuring, I let out a soft mewl as my orgasm overcame me. Resting against the cold tile for a few more minutes, I took some deep breaths before turning off the water. Grabbing a nearby towel, I wrapped myself in it after drying off my body.

Stepping out of the shower, I reached for my bathrobe, but realized I'd left it, along with a change of clothes, in my suitcase which was out in the other room with Blake–the same Blake for whom I'd just done a partial striptease just minutes earlier. Pondering my situation for a moment, I soon realized I had no other option but to ask him for assistance.

Making sure the towel was completely covering my upper body, I opened the door a crack and hollered out to him.

"Blake, can you do me a favor? Can you bring me my big suitcase? I left my clothes out there."

I heard him laugh before answering. "I think that sounds like a personal problem. Maybe if you hadn't been in such a hurry with your exit, you would've remembered. I think you should just come out here wearing only what you were wearing before."

"Please," I begged. "It's getting really cold in here."

"Fine," he huffed.

"Thank you! You can just set it by the door. I'll grab it from there."

"OK," he said, as I heard him get off the bed.

Opening the door a few minutes later, I was surprised to see him staring back at me with his arms folded across his chest.

"Blake! What are you still doing standing here? I'm practically naked!"

Completely ignoring my question, he grinned, asking one of his own. "Why are your cheeks so flushed?"

"They're not!" I insisted.

"Oh, they definitely are. And, come to think of it, I heard something fall when you were in there. What were you doing in the shower?"

"Oh my god! Nothing! I must still be warm from the hot water. That's all."

"I thought you just said you were freezing?" he continued, refusing to let this go. He was trying to embarrass me, and it was working.

"Seriously, are you done? I'd really like to get dressed."

"Don't let me stop you," he added with a wink.

"Alone," I said, stomping my foot.

"Oh, now you're shy?" he asked, raising his brow. "So, let me try and understand. A bra and those cheeky panties are OK, but a cotton towel is not?"

"It was no different than a bikini," I squeaked in defense. Suddenly feeling vulnerable under his intense glare, I wrapped my arms around my chest.

"Whatever you say. I could nearly see your tits through it," he growled into my ear so only I could hear.

Not trusting myself around this man, I took a step back before responding. "I'm sorry. I really don't know what got into me earlier. That was really inappropriate of me." I said, apologetically.

He sniggered before answering, "Please don't feel you need to be appropriate on my account." With that he walked back into the bedroom, allowing me to get dressed. I could tell, I was really in for a long and torturous trip.

After taking a few minutes to regain my composure, I threw on a pair of leggings and my favorite oversized hoodie. I'd already given Blake the wrong impression, and I definitely didn't want to add fuel to the fire by wearing something too sexy. Opening the door into the bedroom, I saw Kaity propped up on several pillows eating a piece of cheese pizza.

"I hope pepperoni is OK?" Blake asked as I walked into the room. "I wasn't really sure what toppings you liked, but I figured everyone likes pepperoni, right?"

"Pepperoni is fine," I said, scooping a few pieces onto a paper plate before joining Kaity on the king-sized bed. "Honestly, I'm so hungry, I probably would've eaten anchovies at this point."

Scrunching up his nose, "So fish eggs are bad, but teeny fish are acceptable? You never fail to surprise me, Cassidy Carpenter."

"Well, I'll take that as a compliment, but I was totally kidding about the anchovies. Those are definitely not acceptable."

Grabbing a few pieces of pizza for himself, Blake turned to look for a place to sit. The only other option besides the bed was an uncomfortable looking office chair in the corner of the room.

"I guess I'll just take a seat over there," he said, pointing toward the chair.

Before I had a chance to suggest otherwise, Kaity piped up. "Don't be silly, Blake. You can't even see the TV from over there. There's plenty of room here between me and Mommy," she said, patting the space between us in bed.

By the look on his face, he was conflicted on whether or not to take her up on the offer. "It's OK, Blake. Come sit with us. You definitely wouldn't want to miss an episode of *Full House* because you're sitting over in the corner. Besides, that chair looks like it'd be a killer on the back," I said, caringly.

"Well, if you insist. After all, *Full House* has always been one of my favorite shows," he said, the bed dipping as he sat.

Kaity's eyes grew in excitement. "Really? It's my favorite show, too! Mommy and I watch it every night. I just love Uncle Jesse," she beamed.

I laughed at her candor. She was just so at ease with Blake. "Like mother, like daughter, I suppose. I've always had a huge crush on John Stamos," I said with a shrug.

"You do? You know I've always thought my hair looks just as good as his," he joked, running his fingers through his thick mane.

"You're so goofy," I said, as soda squirted up my nose. "Now look what you've made me do," I laughed, picking up a pillow and bopping him over the head.

The next thing I knew, pillows were flying and laughter filled the air as the three of us entered into a full-fledged pillow fight.

"That was fun," Kaity giggled. "Can we do it again?"

"Not tonight, Baby. Mommy is too tired," I said, trying to catch my breath. Looking over at Blake, I wasn't surprised to see he hadn't even broken a sweat. The guy was in top physical condition. I couldn't help but peek at his sculpted abs when his shirt rode up during our little pillow fight. He must spend hours in the gym every week.

I wondered for a moment how he was able to raise two children, work a high-pressure job, and spend so much time staying in shape. Did he really have the time to add me, let alone my daughter, into his already busy life?

The three of us watched another episode of *Full House* before Kaity fell asleep sprawled across both of us.

"Well, I suppose I should get going," Blake said, gently lifting Kaity's feet from his legs. "I had a great time with you two tonight."

"Me too," I whispered. "I'll walk you to the door."

"What are your plans tomorrow," he asked before opening the door.

"Actually, I was able to line up a meeting with one of the top bridal gown designers in the city–just as you suggested. I'm meeting him for brunch. After that, I figured Kaity and I would just explore the city until you got home from work."

"I'm actually not working this week. That's something I was hoping to discuss with you. Maybe we can talk about it over dinner tomorrow night?"

"Dinner sounds nice," I said.

"I'd be happy to take Kaity while you're at your appointment. The kids would love it, too," he suggested.

"Oh, I didn't want to impose on you so I already arranged for a reputable sitter through the hotel."

"Cancel it. I'll pick her up around ten, and then I'll drive you to your appointment. Afterwards, we can all explore the city together."

"You drive a hard bargain. I have a feeling you always get your way, don't you?" I asked.

"I do when I set my mind to something," he said, staring right into my eyes.

"Well, I guess we'll see you at ten then," I said, dropping my gaze to the floor.

"I had a great time tonight, Cass," he said, planting a quick kiss on my lips before stepping out of the room.

"Me too," I said, waving as he walked down the hallway toward the bank of elevators.

Turning toward me once more, "I meant what I said, I really did have a great time tonight. Sweet dreams," he said before stepping onto the elevator.

Closing the door behind me, I leaned against it and took a deep breath. The more time I spent with this man, the more I worried that he really would get his way.

Chapter Eight

CASSIDY

SIPPING MY MORNING coffee, I stood by the window looking down at the bustling streets of Manhattan–pedestrians dressed in wool peacoats and wrapped in knitted scarves. If I looked hard enough, I could see their breath in the blustery January air.

Since it was already nearing nightfall when we'd arrived the night before, I hadn't taken the time to enjoy the view outside my window. Savoring a few more minutes of silence, I finished the last sip of coffee before waking Kaity.

"Time to get up, Princess," I said, gently shaking her shoulders. Most children were up before the break of dawn, but not my daughter. Nope, she was a night owl just like her mother. It was going to be a real treat when she'd begin school in the fall.

"Mommy, I don't want to get up. Can't I sleep for ten more minutes?" she argued, flipping onto her side.

"I said to get up. Our friends are going to be here soon, and you need to get dressed if you want to go out and do fun stuff with them today. I think Blake is going to take you to that big park across the street," I said, pointing down toward Central Park.

"Do you think we'll build a snowman like Kristoff and Anna?"

she asked.

"Maybe, but in order to build a snowman, you need to get dressed. Now get up! Go, go, go!" I shouted.

Finally putting her feet on the carpeted floor, she stood and sauntered toward the bathroom.

"Don't forget to brush your teeth," I called after her.

"Mommy, I got this," she sassed. That child was going to be the death of me. She was definitely five going on twenty-five.

As Kaity was finishing in the bathroom, I quickly changed into a pair of skinny jeans and a flowy blouse. Wrapping my hair into a loose bun, I glanced into the mirror before deciding to swipe some rosy gloss across my lips. Staring at my reflection, I was pleased with what I saw. I looked sophisticated, but not over-the-top by any stretch. I looked like someone who was to be taken seriously, even in the big city environment.

Just as I was sliding into my knee-high boots, there was a knock at the door.

"Who is it?" I yelled before opening the door.

"Housekeeping," a male voice announced from the other side.

I'd recognize that deep vibrato anywhere. "Is that so?" I questioned, opening the door. "Do you fluff pillows too?"

"Pillow fluffer extraordinaire," he chuckled.

"Good to know. And, you're right on time," I said, looking down at the silver watch around my wrist. "I must admit, I was a little worried about your punctuality after hearing some stories from Rich."

"You should know better than to believe anything that comes from Rich's mouth," he joked.

"You got me there," I agreed, rolling my eyes.

"Honestly, I'm probably only on time because the kids are still with my parents," he admitted with a shrug.

"Oh, I thought you'd have them by now. I hope Kaity isn't

disappointed. I told her she'd probably get to play with them today."

"Well, I actually have plans to meet them for breakfast after I drop you off for your meeting."

"Oh, OK. Well, I'll just call to see if the sitter is still available then. I just hope she can still get here on time," I said, frustrated that Blake had made plans after he'd told me to cancel the sitter just the night before.

Pulling out my phone, Blake stopped me before I began dialing the childcare service.

"Cass, I think you've misunderstood me. I was planning on taking Kaity to breakfast with us. I told you last night that I would watch her, and I meant that. We'll go have breakfast with my folks, and then we'll go spend some time at Central Park until you're ready for us to come pick you up."

"Oh OK," I said, suddenly overcome with emotion. No man had ever shown my daughter as much attention as Blake had in the last few weeks. Even her own father left us without a fleeting thought. Maybe Blake Mitchell really was what we both needed.

"I'm sorry. I just realized how presumptuous that was of me," he confessed, shaking his head. "I realize now that I should've discussed my plans with you first."

"No, no, it's fine. I think she'll have a great time."

"OK, I really am sorry for not asking you first, though," he said, rocking on his heels as he looked at me.

Suddenly realizing that we were still standing in the doorway, I invited Blake to come inside. "I'm sorry, I don't know why we're still standing out here," I laughed. "Would you like to come in? Kaity seems to be taking forever in the bathroom. I can only imagine what outfit she's chosen for herself today."

"That sounds great," he said, not moving.

"OK, then why are you still standing out there?" I laughed.

"Because I'm staring at those juicy, pink lips. I've wanted to kiss them since I got here, but I'm afraid I'll mess up your make-up," he confessed.

"You can kiss me. I packed plenty of lip gloss," I said, glancing at my purse. "But, why don't you come in first."

"Well in that case," he said, as he stepped into the room and slammed the door behind him.

My pulse quickened as he looked down at me as if he planned to devour me whole.

"Hi," I said, suddenly nervous.

"Hi," he whispered, wrapping his hands behind my neck and pulling me toward him. His lips gently brushed up against mine, a brief tease of what was yet to come. Momentarily pulling away, our mouths just inches apart, he stared at me with dilated eyes.

"You're so beautiful," he groaned, before cupping my cheeks and claiming my mouth. As he skillfully explored my mouth, I breathed in the fresh scent of aftershave mixed with woodsy cologne. My heart rate increasing with each breath I took, I wanted to forget about my work obligations and crawl into bed with Blake. A tiny, little voice brought me back to the present.

"Mommy," I'm ready to go," Kaity said as she skipped out of the bathroom.

Quickly releasing myself from Blake's grip, I turned to face my daughter.

"You look great, Baby. Go put your coat on," I said, trying to recover from Blake's assault on my lips. If he continued to kiss me like this, I was in big trouble.

"Uh, Cass," Blake spoke up beside me. "She's wearing a swimsuit."

"Wait, what?" I questioned, paying closer attention to my daughter's wardrobe. Sure enough, instead of her winter clothes she was prancing around the bedroom wearing a bright pink bathing suit with a frilly, lime-green skirt.

"Baby, why are you wearing your swimsuit? You know it's freezing outside."

"Because you said we were going to do fun things today and swimming is fun. Duh," she quipped.

Placing my hand in front of my face to hide my giggling, I responded. "Go change into a pair of jeans and a sweater, please. You're going out to breakfast with Blake and his parents. I want you to act somewhat civilized."

"What does civil-a-eyes mean?" she asked.

"Child, you're going to send me to an early grave," I laughed. "Now scoot! You're going to make us all late!"

IT'S A GOOD thing Blake drove because there's no way I would've ever made it to my appointment on time. I would've likely given up after the first block, stopped the car, and walked to my destination. I looked at him like he'd grown two heads when he told me that traffic wasn't that bad. According to Blake, it wasn't even rush hour and the traffic was ten times worse than anything I'd ever encountered in my entire life.

With just five minutes to spare, Blake pulled up to the curb to drop me off.

"Are you sure you don't want me to park so we can walk in with you?" he asked for the fifth time.

"No, I think I can handle it. The receptionist told me their office was on the seventh floor. How hard can it be?" I asked, staring up at the immense skyscraper.

"You're positive?" he questioned again.

"Blake! Go! You don't want to keep your parents waiting. They're probably very eager to give you your children back," I said with a smile.

"Fine, but if you need me to come back early, you better call me!"

"You know I will. Thank you," I said, leaning over to give him a peck on the cheek.

Stepping out of the car, I turned to tell Kaitlyn goodbye.

"Bye, Baby," I said, blowing her a kiss. "Be good for Blake, OK."

"Bye, Mommy. I will," she said, returning my kiss.

I stepped onto the curb and waved as Blake pulled back into traffic.

"Cassidy Carpenter is that you?" a female voice called from behind.

"Yes," I said, turning to greet the attractive blond stranger. "And you are?"

"Cass, it's Brynne Riley. We met once back in Michigan at my parent's house," I stared at her for a minute longer, familiarity setting in as she spoke the name I'd tried to forget for the last five years. "I'm Steve's sister."

Suddenly forgetting how to breathe, I continued staring at the woman with my mouth agape, blinking uncontrollably.

"Are you OK," I heard her ask through the ringing in my ears. "You look like you've seen a ghost." Nope, no ghost. Just my past showing up to bring me back to reality just when I was starting to think I could move on, I thought to myself.

"Yes, I'm fine. I just didn't expect to see you here, that's all," I said, my voice barely above a whisper.

"Oh, I've lived here in the city for a few years now. I work in this building at one of the accounting firms. Do you have business here?"

"Yes, I do. With the bridal design studio on the seventh floor," I said, realizing I'd probably revealed too much information.

"Oh, that's great!" she said, seemingly interested. "Was that your husband and daughter I saw dropping you off?"

Not wanting to reveal that her niece was in the car, I decided it was safest to lie about Kaitlyn's genetics. "Oh, no. He's just a friend of mine and that was his daughter."

"Oh, OK, well it was good to see you again, Cass. You know, for what it's worth, I was so mad at my brother when you two broke up. He never did tell us what happened, but we all really loved you. It really is a shame because I doubt he'd be where he is today."

"Nice to see you, too," I lied, hoping she would end this conversation. I didn't have time, and I most certainly didn't want her to start telling me about Steve. Truthfully, I didn't care.

"Well I need to get to work. Maybe, I'll see you around again sometime," she said, waving as she turned and walked toward the building.

Collapsing into the bench beside me, I took several deep breaths, trying to calm my nerves. Looking at my watch, I noticed that I was already several minutes late for my appointment. Pulling out my phone, I considered calling Blake to just come and pick me up.

After my little encounter, I wasn't even sure if I could pull off a work meeting. After all, my being late had probably already ruined any chance of a deal anyways. But, after a few more minutes, I decided that having this business connection could really make some money for my studio. Determined to put my chance meeting with Steve's sister behind me, I got up and resolved to turn this day around.

Chapter Nine

BLAKE

CATCHING ME BY surprise, Kaity reached for my hand as we prepared to cross the street to the restaurant. Even though I'd only known this little girl for a few months, it seemed natural. Like she and her mother were meant to be a part of my life.

I'd hoped Cassidy would've opened up about her relationship with Kaity's father, but so far she hadn't even mentioned his name. I'd casually asked Brooke about him after we'd run into the girls at the diner, but she told me that it wasn't her story to tell. Not wanting to arouse her already growing suspicions about us, I didn't want to press any further.

All I'd determined, from Cassidy's fear of commitment along with passing comments, was that he was no longer a part of their lives. I understood that sometimes a relationship between two people doesn't last for whatever reason, but what I could never comprehend was how a father could abandon his child. I'd only been a father for two years, but in that space of time those two children had become my reason for being.

Walking into the diner, Kaity let go of my hand and ran to the booth the minute she spotted Maddy and Ben.

"Hi Maddy! Hi Ben!" she said, excitedly. "Oh, and hi people I don't know!" she added, turning to look at my parents.

"Well, hello there, Darling. Do you have a name?" Mom asked before taking a sip of coffee.

"My name is Kaitlyn Carpenter. I'm almost five. I live at 134—," she said, my mom stopping her before she could finish. I chuckled, remembering that was the same way she'd introduced herself to me several weeks earlier.

"Well it's nice to meet you, Kaitlyn. My name is Penny and this is Dennis," she said, pointing toward my father who had his head buried in the stock pages of the *Times*. "We're Maddy and Ben's grandma and grandpa."

Kaity's eyes widened before she responded enthusiastically. "Oh, I have a grandma and grandpa back home in Michigan. I call them Geema and Geepa! Can I call you Geema and Geepa too?"

Catching us both off guard, my mom looked at me for permission before answering Kaitlyn. Not knowing exactly how to respond, I nodded my head giving her my blessing. Admittedly, even though I was still Blake, I had thought about the idea of Kaitlyn calling me Dad in the future as well.

"I like the sound of that very much. What about you, Geepa?" she asked my dad.

"Uh huh, great," he responded, putting the stocks down for a moment.

Kaity scooted into the booth to sit next to Maddy and my mother while I took a seat next to Ben and my dad.

"So, tell me about Kaitlyn's mother," my mother asked, getting right to the point.

"You never were one to ask the easy questions were you Mom?" I chuckled as a waitress walked up to our table.

"Are you ready to order, or would you like a few more minutes?" she asked, setting a pitcher of water on the table.

"I think we're ready," I said, always ordering the same item. "I'll have the usual: three-egg omelet special with bacon and an English muffin, and two orders of waffles and sausage with three plates for the kids, please."

My parents placed their orders, and I was once again left alone with Mom's question lingering over us.

"So, who is she, Blake? She must be pretty important to you if you're bringing her daughter along for a family breakfast," she said, pointing toward the girls who were busily coloring on their place mats.

Exhaling deeply, I answered, "Her name is Cassidy Carpenter. I met her at Rich's wedding. She's Brooke's, his wife's, best friend."

"Didn't they get married months ago?" Mom asked, seemingly shocked that this was the first time she was hearing of this.

"It's been a few months, yes," I said. "We haven't been seeing each other that long, though. Cass was hesitant at first. Truthfully, she still is."

"Rightfully so," my mother agreed.

"Mom, please. I don't need the lecture. I'm over thirty. I think I know what's best for me. You can stop mothering me."

"I'll always be your mom, Blake. It's not something that you can just turn off. You'll understand when Maddy and Ben are older and they start dating. You'll want to lock them away in their rooms and never let them come out."

"She's good for me, Mom," I said, trying to reassure her. "I know it. I just wish she knew it too."

"So, she lives in Michigan then?" Mom asked.

"Yeah, she does," I nodded.

"And, you're OK with a long-distance relationship with this girl? Because she probably has a life there that she may not want to leave, Blake. And, you can't be uprooting your kids, either. They've already been through so much."

I sighed in relief when I noticed the waitress approaching our table once again. I didn't have it in me to discuss my future living situation any further. Digging into my food, I said a silent prayer that my mother would just let it go–at least for now.

We'd made it through breakfast without any more discussion of my relationship status, only two dirty-diaper changes, and one spilled chocolate milk. All in all, I considered the morning quite a success. Reaching for the check, Mom swatted my hand away before I had a chance to pick it up.

"I got it," she said, smiling. "It's not every day that I get to treat my son and grandchildren to breakfast."

"Thanks, Mom," I said with a half-smile. "I know I don't say it enough, but I really do appreciate everything you've both done especially since we lost Alyssa."

"We know, Son. And, I'm sorry if I said too much about your new friend. I just worry about you is all. I just want you to be happy, and I don't want to see you get hurt. Lord knows, you've already suffered through a lifetime of hurt."

Swallowing back my emotion, I responded. "It's been difficult, but, truth is, the day I met Cass, my days began to get a bit brighter."

"Well, then, if she's responsible for putting that smile back on my son's face then that's good enough for me. She's definitely raised a terrific little girl," she said, nodding toward Kaity who was now busily teaching Maddy how to play a game of tic-tac-toe.

"Yes, that she has," I said, smiling.

Just as I was preparing to bundle the kids back into their snow gear so we could head to Central Park, my phone alerted me to an incoming text.

Cassidy: My meeting wasn't actually as long as I was expecting. They were already familiar with my work, and we came to an agreement rather quickly! I'm ready for you to come and get me.

Blake: OK, we're still at the restaurant. We'll be there in a few minutes. Sit tight.

Cassidy: Oh! I don't want to interrupt your time with your parents! I'll just go and sit in the coffee shop that I noticed down the street.

McPherson's. I knew the place well. Not wanting to set foot in there again, I had to keep Cass out of there, too.

Blake: Actually, we were just finishing up. Just wait in the lobby, and we'll be there in five. You can go with us to the park.

Cassidy: OK, see you soon! :)

My parents helped get the kids fastened into their car seats, before saying our goodbyes.

"I hope I get to meet Cassidy soon, Son," my mom said, giving me a kiss on the cheek.

"I hope so, too, Mom," I said, pulling her in for an embrace.

"You know, Son, for what it's worth, I know your mother thinks you may be moving too quickly, but you just can't put a timetable on your life. If Cassidy makes you happy then we're both happy for you," my dad interjected.

"Thanks, Pops," I said, patting him on the back. My father was a man of few words, but when he spoke I always listened. He'd always given me sound advice, and had always been there when my mom and I needed him. I'd always said that if I could be half the father that he's been to my brother and me then I'd be doing a fine job.

Waving goodbye, I slid into my car, and pulled out into traffic.

PULLING UP TO the curb, I noticed Cass sitting on a park-style bench waiting for us–her bright pink coat sticking out like a sore thumb even in New York City. Beeping the horn, she turned in our direction.

"Hey, Beautiful, can we give you a lift?" I called out the window.

"Well, I don't usually accept a ride from strangers, but you don't look so dangerous," she laughed, already walking toward the car.

"Only in the bedroom," I mumbled, as she opened the passenger door.

"You really don't ever stop, do you? I didn't think it was possible, but I truly believe I've met my match in you," she said, blushing when she thought about the words she'd spoken. "I mean . . ."

"Relax, Cass. I knew what you meant," I insisted. "Now what do you all say we head to the park?"

"Sounds great to me," she said, turning toward the back seat. "What do you kids think?"

"Yay!" the girls squealed, and Ben let out an excited cry.

"I think that's an affirmative from the peanut gallery," she laughed.

TAKING OVER AN empty bench, Cass and I watched as Kaity took control of the show and began teaching Maddy the how-to of snowman building. Luckily, the day had turned sunny and was getting warmer. Ben was comfortably sleeping beside me in his blanket-covered stroller.

At thirteen months, he hadn't quite learned the art of walking yet. Maddy had been up and running around at ten months, but with Ben being a preemie, he was a bit behind his sister. The doctors were all pleased with his development though and I was sure that within no time he'd be up and chasing after his sister.

"Kaity really has seemed to take Maddy under her wing," I said, watching as the girls began rolling two giant snowballs.

"Don't get too carried away now. My daughter just likes having someone to boss around and Maddy is pretty much putty in her hands," Cass laughed, shaking her head.

Keeping my eyes fixed on the girls, I also wanted to use this time to have a meaningful conversation with Cass. Instead of diving in right away with the hard questions, I thought I would take a softer approach and hope we could work our way up from there.

"So, tell me about your meeting? You signed the deal?"

"Yep," she said. "Like I told you over text, they'd been following me for a while so it really wasn't a hard sell."

"That's great! Anything interesting happen during your discussion?"

"No, not really. Thankfully, my little encounter before I'd even entered the building didn't seem to have an effect. I felt so jittery, but it didn't even seem like Mr. Curtis noticed."

"What do you mean? Who did you run into?" I asked confusedly.

"Um," she paused, seemingly hesitant to finish her story.

"Cass, please."

Exhaling, she answered, "Steve's sister."

Shaking my head in confusion, "I still don't understand. Who's Steve?"

"My ex. Kaitlyn's father," she confessed.

Cocking my head, I continued. "But, I thought her father lived in Michigan? Why is his sister here?"

"Would you believe that she works in the same building? She said she moved to New York a few years ago," she sighed.

"Does that mean that Steve is here too?" I asked, glancing

toward the girls who had now moved on to collecting sticks for their snowman's arms.

"I don't know. I didn't ask. I didn't really want to know," she said, balling her hands into tight fists.

"Did she ask about Kaitlyn?"

"No," she nodded. "It didn't seem like she knew anything about her. She noticed her in the car, but I just explained that we were friends and she was your daughter. I'm sorry I got you messed up in a lie, but I don't really want him trying to come back into her life now. I know my little girl deserves a father, but he doesn't deserve her. I hope that doesn't sound too selfish of me. I'm just trying to protect her."

"Cass," I said, placing my hand on her shoulder. "I get it completely. I want to protect her too." Biting the inside of her cheek, I could tell she was fighting back tears.

Taking the plunge, I asked her the question that had been lying heavily on my mind. "Why did he leave?"

"He left the day I found out I was pregnant. He found me hovered and heaving over the toilet. He called me a slut and told me I was going to get fat, and then he walked out of our lives. I haven't seen him since," she said, tears falling down her cheeks.

My hands tightening into fists, I wanted nothing more than to find the jackass and pound his face into a brick wall. Pulling Cass into my chest, I held her firmly for a few minutes until her tears began to subside.

"I'm sorry," she said, wiping her face with the back of her hand. "This isn't like me. But, seeing her today just brought it all back."

"Don't be sorry, Cass. Don't ever be sorry around me," I said, reassuringly.

"I'm just so scared," she admitted. "What if he comes back? What if he wants to see her?"

Looking toward Kaity and then back to her mother, I made a promise to them both. "As long as I'm in your life, Steve won't be a problem. I'll make sure of it," I vowed. In that moment, I wasn't sure how I could possibly keep that promise, but I knew I needed to try–for all of us.

Chapter Ten

BLAKE

*N*EARING LATE AFTERNOON, the girls still hadn't finished their snowman. They'd been distracted several times as they stopped to pet nearly every dog that came along the path and used every spot of clean snow to create tiny, little snow angels. Knowing Maddy would need a nap before dinner, I decided I'd quickly help them finish.

"Looks like you girls still need a nose, eyes, and hat on that thing," I said, walking toward them.

"He's not a thing, Blake. He's Olaf!" Kaity yelled, crossing her arms across her chest. She was definitely as feisty as her mother.

Hearing Cass giggling in the distance was like music to my ears. I had to keep up the charade with Kaity a little longer. "Olaf, huh? What kind of name is Olaf?"

Kaity's eyes grew as she spoke, "He's from Frozen! It's only the best movie ever made!"

"He knows, Baby. I think Blake was just kidding you," Cass yelled from the bench, as Ben bounced on her lap sucking on some Cheerios. She seemed so natural with him–with both of my kids. All three of us were starting to fall for her, and for Kaity too.

"Ohhhhh OK. You're real funny, Blake," Kaity said, interrupting my thoughts.

"Sorry, Princess. Will you forgive me?"

"Of course!" Kaity said, wrapping her tiny arms around my waist.

"Good! Now what do you say we find Olaf here some eyes and a nose?"

"I think he'd like that very much," she agreed, bopping her head up and down.

"How about buttons for his eyes? It just so happens I have a few extra ones sewn on the inside of my coat," I said, carefully pulling off the spare buttons on the interior lining of my coat. Who knew those replacement buttons would ever come in handy?

"Olaf!" Maddy squealed, clapping her hands.

"And, how about a pencil for a nose? It just so happens that I have an extra one here in my pocket," he said, patting Maddy on the head. I suppose carrying extra pencils and pens around came with being a journalist. You never knew when your next story might strike.

"Here Maddy, do you want to help me stick Olaf's nose on?" Kaity asked Maddy, grabbing her hand.

Not exactly knowing what we could use for a hat, I took a quick look around the park to see if I could spot anything. Atop one of the trash bins, I noticed a round popcorn tub. It wasn't exactly the right color, but it would definitely work as a hat.

Feeling Cass's eyes on me as I walked to the trash can, I turned in her direction. "Are you staring at my butt," I asked.

"Hardly! I just can't believe you're about to go Dumpster diving for a 'hat,'" she said, using air quotes.

"It's not exactly a Dumpster, and it's right on top!" I yelled, grabbing the container.

"OK, well while you dig for garbage, I'm going to go find a lady's room."

"There are plenty of shops near the entrance where we came in. Do you want me to walk with you? We can all go," I said, as she began packing up our things.

"No, it's fine. Help the girls finish Olaf, and take plenty of pictures. I've got Ben. I think the big guy can use another diaper change anyways. We'll meet you back at the car in fifteen minutes?" she asked, checking the time on her watch.

Just as Cass had instructed, the girls and I finished Olaf, rounding out his ensemble by tying my black scarf around his neck. I had another one at home so parting with this one wasn't really such a big deal. I even packed a bit more snow around his midsection so he wouldn't look quite so skinny. Once we were pleased with the final product, the three of us then gathered around Olaf as I snapped a few selfies, immediately texting them off to Cass. A few seconds later, my phone dinged with a reply.

> Cass: Well isn't that just adorable! I must admit, the popcorn tub-hat adds a nice touch. I don't often admit when I'm wrong, so kudos to you, Mr. Mitchell. ;)

> Blake: So, you'll know, I just took a screenshot of that. Now I'll have permanent proof of your admitting that you were wrong.

> Cass: I'm sure you did. Anyways, I went into that cute little coffee shop that I mentioned earlier. You should meet us here. They have the cutest little kids' area, and I bet Kaity would love some hot chocolate.

Knowing I wasn't ready to step back into McPherson's, I had to get Cass and Ben out of there without alerting her that something was wrong.

> Blake: I don't think that's such a good idea. I can already tell that

Maddy is getting pretty grumpy. I really should get her down for a nap. We'll just meet you at the car like we already agreed.

Cass: Oh, come on, Dad! Surely, she'll be fine for a little longer. I'm sure a little hot chocolate will perk her up. After all, chocolate cures everything, even a little case of the grumps. We'll wait for you by the fireplace.

Realizing I wasn't going to win this battle, I agreed to meet her. I just hoped my heart would be able to handle it. Walking into McPherson's was like stepping into a time warp. Not noticing Cass sitting with Ben by the fire, or the girls running to them, I was immediately transported back a decade earlier when I'd first set eyes on Alyssa.

Having a few extra minutes to spare before I hopped on the subway to my grad class at Columbia, I ducked into a small coffee beanery about ten minutes from the station in hopes of grabbing a cup of java before my first class.

Walking through the door, my eyes were immediately drawn to the barista serving drinks behind the counter. Her honey blond hair fanned out on her shoulders and her sapphire eyes sparkled as she turned to face me. The white company T-shirt she wore hugged her natural curves in all the right places causing my cock to twitch with desire.

"Hi, welcome to McPherson's. May I take your order?" she asked, as I approached the counter. Her voice was silky-smooth, and in that moment I wanted nothing more than to hear her scream my name in bed. I couldn't help it, I was a twenty-two-year-old man. I pretty much had four needs: beer, food, sports, and sex.

"Yes, Alyssa," I said, reading her name tag—giving me a reason to check out her ample rack. "I'd just like a large coffee with two creams and two sugars, please."

"Will that be all? Could I interest you in an almond scone? It's a

house recipe."

"If I say yes, can I have your number too?" I asked. I'd never been shy around the ladies, and I sure as hell wasn't about to start now.

"Ummm, I have a boyfriend," she stuttered, as if I'd suddenly made her nervous. I'd almost bet by her sudden shyness that she didn't actually have a boyfriend, but I'd just caught her off-guard.

"I'll wait," I said, winking.

"So just the coffee then? That'll be three dollars and seventeen cents," she said, ignoring my advances.

Not wanting to be late for my first class, I paid for my coffee. "Thanks for the Joe. I'll see you tomorrow, Alyssa," I said, turning to leave.

"I don't work tomorrow," she said.

"Well, I'll see you the day after that then," I said with a smile. "Unless, of course, I can see you tonight for dinner?"

She giggled before answering, "Boyfriend, remember?"

"Sticking to that story then?" I asked, watching her cheeks redden as she exhaled sharply. Judging from her lack of response, I knew I'd been right. "Day after tomorrow it is then," I said, as I walked out the door and headed toward campus.

I'd sat through my first two classes with nothing but a gorgeous, blond barista on the brain. A woman had never quite affected me in the same way as Alyssa had. I was still young, and definitely not in search of a permanent relationship. But, when I saw her, it just felt different— unexplainable, really.

Walking into my last class for the day—media law, I was shocked to see the girl from the coffee shop sitting right in the front row. She was rummaging through her backpack and didn't notice me as I approached from behind.

"Excuse me, Alyssa, but is this seat taken?" I asked.

"How do you know my name?" she asked, looking up at me. "Oh, it's you."

"Not quite the response I was looking for, but at least you remember *me," I chuckled. "I don't believe I properly introduced myself earlier, I'm Blake Mitchell," I added, extending my hand to her.*

"Alyssa Turner," she said, reaching for my hand.

"It's a pleasure to meet you, Alyssa Turner. Is it OK if I sit here next to you?" I asked her again.

"It's fine," she said, her cheeks flushing again.

"What brings the pretty barista into a media law class at Columbia? Are you in the journalism graduate program, too?" I inquired, interested in learning more about her.

She bit her lip before answering, "I'm only working at McPherson's to help with the bills. I'm actually a law student here. Today's my first day in the program."

"A lawyer, huh?" I responded, picturing her standing in a courtroom wearing a tight skirt, button-down shirt which just exposed a minimal amount of cleavage, glasses, and her long, blond hair wrapped into a loose bun. Shifting slightly in my seat, I grabbed my bag and sat it on my lap to hide my now throbbing, bulging dick. When I first saw Alyssa sitting in the lecture hall, I thought I might be able to focus better in this class. Boy, had I been wrong. Leaving the class, I only hoped with her sitting next to me that I wouldn't fail the entire semester.

"Blake, over here," I heard Cassidy speak.

"Daddy! Hot chocolate?" Maddy asked, tugging on my sleeve.

Pinching the bridge of my nose, I tried to put the memories of this place in the past where they belonged.

"Sure, Kiddo, we can get hot chocolate," I said, walking toward Cass, who was sitting by the fireplace enjoying her beverage.

"Are you OK? You look like you've seen a ghost," she said, as I took a seat next to her.

"Yeah, I'm fine. Just tired. Snowman building can really wear a guy out," I said with a fake laugh. Truthfully, I'd hardly broken a sweat. I just didn't want Cass to know the real reason for my sudden mood change.

Sitting by the fire as Cass took the girls to order hot chocolates, I gazed into the flames as more memories of this place flooded my mind.

Autumn in New York, quickly turned into winter and I still hadn't convinced Alyssa to go out with me–not on a proper date, anyways. The closest we came to a date was studying together each night at McPherson's after she finished her shifts. We'd grab the booth in the corner and sit there until late into the night going over our course work.

Once we'd finished our assignments in media law for the day, I'd sit there even longer and help her with her other courses–leaving mine until I got home each night. I didn't get much sleep, but spending time with Alyssa was worth it–and, honestly, the highlight of most of my days. The girl had me by the balls, and she didn't even realize it.

Sitting at my favorite table, I couldn't take my eyes off her has she wiped down the counter, her tits dragging across the surface as she stretched to reach the farthest corner. On more than one occasion, I'd fantasized about slowly stripping her bare and spreading her out on that same counter.

I hadn't even kissed her yet, but I knew her mouth and her pussy were made just for me. Reaching under the table, I readjusted my junk, reminding myself that it would be several more hours before I could relieve the ache between my thighs. If I had to keep jacking myself off every night, I would have to start going to the gym just to strengthen my left arm to keep up with the increased workout my right had been getting lately.

Catching me staring at her, she smiled and waved before bringing out the coffeepot to refill my mug for the millionth time.

"You know, if you stay for much longer, I'm going to have to charge you for another coffee," she giggled. "That's not true, that says free refills," I said, pointing toward the chalkboard sign that hung on the back wall.

"True, but most customers only stay for a few hours–max. You've

been here since I started my shift this morning! They really should just put you on payroll," she sassed.

"Agree to have dinner with me then, and I won't sit here all day," I suggested.

"But, what if I like your sitting here all day?" she admitted, looking down and picking a piece of lint off her apron.

"What if I still sat here all day, and then took you out to dinner?" I propositioned.

"I think, maybe, I'd like that," she said, her mouth curving into a smile.

"I know just the perfect place. How about you give me your address, and I'll pick you up Friday night at seven."

Chapter Eleven

CASSIDY

ATER ORDERING THE girls' hot chocolates, Blake insisted we leave right away. I tried to get him to relax just a little longer by the fire, but he refused, adamant that the kids needed naps before dinner. I thought he'd open up once we returned to the car, but instead we sat in silence for several lingering minutes.

Wishing I knew what caused the sudden shift between us, I decided to broach the subject. Noticing his hand resting on the gearshift, I gently placed mine on top of his. Glancing in my direction, he forced a half-smile.

"Hey, you OK over there?" I asked, breaking the deafening silence. "You're not the same guy you were while we were at the park."

"Yep, I'm fine," he said, returning his attention back to the road. "Just tired."

"You sure? It seemed like something happened back there. Was it something I said?"

"I said I'm fine, Cass. Let it go, OK?" he snapped, twisting his wedding band as it rested against the wheel. Something was definitely not right. In the time I'd known Blake, he'd never once raised his voice–especially with his children within earshot. Not wanting to get into it with him in front of the kids, I removed my hand from his, and agreed to let it go, but it would be on my terms.

"Yeah, OK," I nodded, my frustration growing. "You can just take Kaity and me back to the hotel."

"No, we're having dinner at my place. We agreed on this earlier and I already bought groceries. I was planning on cooking for you two," he said, tension still evident in his tone.

"I just thought you might want to be alone, that's all. We can have dinner some other time. It's not a big deal."

"It's a big deal to me. We're having dinner at my place–tonight. End of discussion. Besides, you're leaving in the morning."

There was no use arguing with him. If there was anything I'd learned about Blake in the short time that we'd been together was that he was determined and as stubborn as a mule. I sighed, just hoping he would start talking over dinner, or I wasn't sure if I could keep opening myself up to him.

Blake went ahead of me into the apartment, immediately taking the kids to their bedrooms with Kaity following closely behind. Walking into his apartment, I was momentarily surprised by its homey décor. It was nothing like the bachelor pad that I'd envisioned with stark white walls, and bare hardwood floors. It was quite the opposite, actually, with chocolaty-brown walls and sandy, plush carpeting that squished under my toes.

The furniture looked plush and inviting–like I could crawl onto the couch and take a nap, covering myself with the fuzzy throw which draped the back. On the walls hung colorful abstract art. It was almost as if his home revealed a woman's touch.

Glancing over toward the mantel, I was struck with a gentle reminder that his home did have a woman's touch–Alyssa's touch. A row of family portraits lined the shelf–newborn pictures of

Maddy and Ben as well as a bridal portrait of Alyssa. She was simply stunning, wearing a gorgeous cream chiffon gown, with a white lace overlay, fitted-bodice with flecks of gold threaded throughout. It was a Vera Wang; I remembered the dress vividly from many seasons earlier. It was exquisite on each of my brides who tried it on, and Alyssa was no exception. Her long, blond hair twisted to the side in a loose French braid, a few tendrils curling at the side, a simple strand of cream pearls resting on her collar. Her bouquet of red roses was simple yet elegant.

Setting the bridal portrait back on the mantel, I picked up another picture which sat next to it. This one of Blake, Alyssa, and Maddy running down the beach, the sun beginning to set in the distance. Maddy looked to be about a year old, barely able to walk without assistance as her two parents flung her up in the air between them–Alyssa with a very rounded, pregnant belly. They looked happy. They looked in love. They were a beautiful, growing family.

Blake's apartment definitely wasn't a typical bachelor pad. This apartment was decorated by a woman for her family–Blake and Alyssa's family. I suddenly felt out of place–as though I were invading another woman's domain. Just as I was about to set the picture back down, I felt Blake's presence behind me.

"That was taken just a few weeks before . . ." he trailed off before finishing his thought.

"Do you want to talk about her?" I asked, realizing we'd never talked much about Alyssa or her death. Everything I knew coming from Brooke.

"No," he said, his tone showing zero emotion.

"Blake, I'd really love to know more about her. Please tell me." I nearly begged.

"Please put the picture down. I have dinner ready in the kitchen," he said, turning his back toward me, ignoring my request completely.

"Why are you shutting me out now? Especially after I opened up about Steve earlier? Do you have any idea how hard that was for me?"

"I do, but I just don't want to talk about her," he said, an agonizing growl coming from deep inside his chest. "Please just drop it," he asked again, slamming his fist against the kitchen counter. The expression worn on his face was pained, tormented even. Though I tried to understand his frustration, I wasn't sure I could endure his sorrow when I couldn't even heal my own scars.

Suddenly the walls felt like they were closing in on me. Blake was cold. He wasn't the same man I'd been falling for just hours earlier as he built a snowman with the kids. He'd been replaced with a shell of a man whom I hardly recognized. Sure, he looked the same on the outside, but it's as if everything on the inside had turned him into the same men whom I'd spent the last five years trying to avoid.

"I thought you were different," I yelled, my eyes swimming with unshed tears. "I finally let you in just for you to close me off!"

"I'm sorry. I don't know what else to say other than I'm sorry. I didn't mean to hurt you, but I guess I'm just not as ready for all of this as I thought I was," he confessed, conflict evident in his face as he once again twisted the ring on his finger as if it were burning his skin.

"Why don't you just take it off?" I asked.

"Take what off?" he asked, confused by my comment.

"Your wedding ring. You're constantly fidgeting with it like it's hurting you. Maybe it's time to take it off."

"I was considering it until you brought it up. I won't feel pressured into saying goodbye. I told her I'd never say goodbye," he snarled, painfully.

"I wasn't asking you to say goodbye, Blake," I said, biting my lip trying to hold back the tears.

He didn't respond, but just stood there expressionless. "You know what, it doesn't really matter. I'm really not very hungry. I think I'll just call for an Uber to take us back to the hotel," I said, wiping a stray tear from my eye. "Goodbye, Blake." The irony wasn't lost on me that even though Blake couldn't tell Alyssa goodbye that he'd let me say the word without so much as a fight.

DRAGGING KAITY OUT of Maddy's room while they were in the middle of playing tea party wasn't one of my proudest moments as a mother. I shouldn't have taken my daughter to New York. I shouldn't have introduced her to Blake or his children in the first place. Deep down, I knew it wouldn't work. Maybe if we'd met in a different lifetime we could've survived, but not now. We both had too many demons weighing us down.

Now I was tasked with explaining to my daughter why she couldn't see Blake or her friends anymore.

"Are we going back to Blake's house tomorrow, Mommy?" Kaity asked, arriving back at the hotel.

"No, Baby. We're leaving in the morning. Mommy has to work, but you'll get to see Aunt Brookie and Uncle Rich. You'll like that, right?"

"Yeah, but I'll miss my new friends," she pouted. "I know, Kaity, but you have friends back at home, too. You like our new neighbor, Natalie, right?"

"Yeah, she's fun!" Kaity beamed, suddenly forgetting why she was upset in the first place. "She has a lot of fun games!" If only adults were as resilient as children–my heart wouldn't feel like it was cracking into a million, tiny pieces right now.

After tucking Kaity in for the night, I held my phone for a moment, contemplating calling Brooke. She was the only person who understood me. She'd be able to talk me off this ledge I was teetering on.

I just knew she'd be devastated that I hadn't told her about Blake or New York sooner. I mean, I was pretty sure she knew, but hearing the words come from my mouth would be different. I was supposed to be her best friend. We'd made a pact as kids to never keep secrets from each other. I just prayed that in this mess with Blake, I hadn't ruined our friendship along the way.

Deciding to tell Brooke face to face about my relationship with Blake, I scrolled past her name and landed on his. Wanting to know if he was OK, I dialed his number, but quickly hung up before even allowing it to ring. I knew I'd hurt him when I left, pure anguish written on his face. But, by not opening up, he'd hurt me too–especially given the skeletons that I'd revealed earlier in the day.

Not even bothering to change into my pajamas, I fell asleep in the glow of the television. Waking up shortly before dawn, I reached for my phone, assuming I'd missed a call or text from Blake. Nothing. Exhaling deeply, I knew it was really over between us. I guess I wouldn't have to worry about the logistics of a long-distance relationship after all.

As I was packing the last of our things, there came a knock at the door. Surprised that the driver I'd hired the night before hadn't called first, I checked the peephole before answering. Shocked to see Blake standing in the hallway, I hesitated a few moments before opening the door.

"Blake," I said, surprise evident in my voice. "I didn't expect to see you here. I don't have much time. We're leaving soon. The driver should be here shortly to take us to the airport." Looking over toward Kaity, I was relieved when I saw she was engrossed in her headphones and iPad, not even seeing that Blake was here with us.

"I know. I just need a few minutes. I couldn't let you leave before I had a chance to see you again."

"You could've just called," I suggested, not letting on that his presence was having an effect on me."

"I could've, but I wasn't so sure you'd answer, and that wasn't a chance I was willing to take," he confessed, rubbing his forehead.

"Oh, I guess I have a few minutes then," I said, letting him enter the room. Noticing for the first time that he was alone, I wondered about the kids. "Where are Maddy and Ben?"

"With my mom."

"At this hour," I asked, surprised that she'd have the kids before seven o'clock in the morning.

"I called and told her I had a work emergency so she came right over. I have a feeling she suspected otherwise, but I'll deal with her later," he confessed.

"OK," I nodded in understanding. "Do you want to sit?" I asked, gesturing to the corner of the bed.

"Look, Cass, I'm sorry for getting so upset back at the house," he said, taking a seat. "It's just that the coffee shop you went into holds too many memories for me. It's where I first met Alyssa."

Stunned that he was telling me all of this now, I sat there for a moment in silence before answering. "Oh, I'm so sorry. Why didn't you just tell me? I would've left right away had I known it was that difficult for you."

"I thought being with you would change things," he admitted. "I thought it would be bearable. When in reality, it actually felt worse–like I was cheating on her. Then I felt like I was cheating on you because I was thinking about her."

"I just want to know a little about her. I don't need to know all her personal details. I just want to know one thing about her, then maybe tomorrow two more things."

He chuckled softly before responding, "OK, then, I know just the story to start with. On our first date, I took her to one of the most expensive restaurants in the city. I'd put money aside for weeks in order to pay for it. It had taken her so long to finally agree to go on a date with me that I wanted to make it special.

"When the waiter came to take our order, I was shocked when all she wanted was the mac and cheese off the kids' menu. She could've ordered lobster tails, or filet mignon and instead chose a dish off the kids' menu," he laughed, shaking his head.

"Honestly, that sounds like something I would do," I giggled. "Although, I would probably go for the grilled cheese."

"I don't know where things stand between us, but I'm not willing to let you go. Please stay for another day. We can explore the city, and have dinner tonight since I messed it up last night," he asked.

"I would love to, but my tickets are for today. I have to go," I said, suddenly wishing I could change my flight.

"You can change your flight. I bought the added travel insurance when I booked the tickets. We'll just tell them that something came up with your work, and you need to stay another day."

"Well, OK, then. I guess you have us for another day," I agreed, curling my mouth into a half smile, and giving Blake a peck on the cheek. "Just promise to not shut me out if something gets hard."

"Deal," he sighed, pulling me in closer. I was at least confident to see where the day would take us.

Chapter Twelve

CASSIDY

*J*UST AS BLAKE had promised, he took Kaity on a Fifth Avenue shopping spree which included a stop at the American Girl store, where she picked out a brand-new doll and matching wardrobe. And, since I was along for the ride, I decided to take a detour myself and ended up perusing the aisles of Saks Fifth Avenue where I snatched up a pair of shoes and matching handbag. When in New York, right? For lunch, we'd stopped for corn dogs and falafels at two of the city's most iconic food trucks.

Before heading back to the hotel, we made a final stop at the infamous Serendipity where we indulged on frozen hot chocolates and ordered a few other sweet treats to go. Blake and I took a seat at a bistro-style table for two while he gave Kaity several quarters to play a claw-style arcade game across the room. He was already spoiling her rotten.

"This is one of my favorite movies ever," I sighed, remembering the film that shared the restaurant's name.

"I don't think I've ever seen it," Blake admitted.

"How is that even possible? It's like only the most romantic movie ever made!" I said, exuberantly.

He chuckled, turning toward me, a grin wide across his lips.

"What's so funny?" I asked, shaking my head.

"You just don't seem like the hopeless romantic type, that's all. I pegged you for more of a traditional comedy girl. You know, like, *Animal House, Old School,* and *Wedding Crashers?*" he said jokingly.

"Well, those are all fine movies, but don't forget my profession. I'll always be a romantic at heart, even if I don't believe in my own fairy tale," I said, sadness in my voice.

"I'll turn you into a believer yet, Carpenter," he whispered, almost inaudibly.

"Do you believe in serendipity?" I asked, staring at the flashing sign in the window.

"Not really," he confessed. "I guess I'm more of a realist. I believe that everything in life happens for a reason, and we need to take action and go after things that we want before it's too late. The last year has definitely taught me that," he said.

"Hmmm," I sighed. "Maybe if you watch the movie, you'll change your mind. I really can't believe you've never seen it. We'll definitely have to correct that sometime."

"That sounds like a great idea. It only means you want to spend more time with me," he said with a smile. "After last night, I wasn't so sure that was the case."

"Today's a new day," I said, reaching out and squeezing his hand.

"You're right about that. What do you say we have dinner tonight? Just the two of us?" Blake asked as he continued holding my hand. "I'd like to try again after last night. Let me cook for you?"

"What about Kaity? I believe the child care service the hotel recommended is only available during the daytime."

"I'm sure my folks will watch her. They already have my kids. They really took to her yesterday."

Hesitating for a moment, I finally agreed to let him ask them. "It's all set. Mom agreed to watching all three kids so we can have dinner tonight," Blake said, ending his call. "She said we could drop Kaity off now if we'd like."

"At their house?" I questioned, surprised that he wanted to take me to his parents' home.

"Yeah, is that OK?"

"I just–I just don't think I'm ready to meet your parents, Blake. I mean, I'm sure they're lovely people, but this is all just moving really quickly for me. That's all," I said, panic beginning to set in. I hadn't met another man's parents since I met Steve's family all those many years ago. Since then, it'd been a step I'd been unwilling to take.

"It's OK, Cass. You're right. I shouldn't even have mentioned it. Why don't I take you back to the hotel and you can get ready for dinner? I'll drop Kaity off before I come back and pick you up?" Blake suggested.

Taking a minute to let it all soak in, I finally agreed to his plan. "I think that sounds great. Thanks for being so understanding," I said with a half-smile.

REALIZING WE WERE alone together for the first time without any kids as a buffer, I took a deep breath to calm my nerves. I wasn't sure why I was so anxious about spending the evening with Blake as he was only making me dinner.

"Can I pour you a glass of wine while I get dinner ready," he asked as I hopped up on a kitchen stool.

"Sure, I'd love some," I answered as he opened the small wine cooler in the corner of the room.

"Red or white?" he asked, pulling both a bottle of Moscato and Merlot from the shelf.

"White, please," I answered, as grabbed the bottle, popping the cork. "What's for dinner?"

Assuming he was preparing something like spaghetti, I was taken aback by his response. "Steak with a mushroom tequila sauce, twice-baked potatoes, and grilled asparagus with a lemon butter glaze," he said, smiling.

"Aren't you fancy? Where'd you learn to cook all that?" I asked, surprise in my voice.

"Actually, I taught myself," he said, exhaling sharply. "After Alyssa and I were married, she still had a year left of school before she finished her law degree. We didn't have much money so I watched a lot of cooking shows so we didn't have to live off Ramen. I learned how to cook fancier dishes on a dime."

"You're just full of surprises. What other hidden talents do you possess?" I asked, truly interested in learning more about him.

"I know how to load a dishwasher," he laughed.

"Wow, you cook and do dishes? Tell me you can do laundry, and I think you might just be the perfect man."

"I can, but sometimes I mix colors with the whites," he cackled.

"You're such a rebel," I giggled.

"What about you? Do any cooking?" he asked.

"I can hold my own in a kitchen. After all, I did live with Brooke while we were in college, and that girl can't cook to save her life. I, honestly, don't know how Rich survives," I laughed. "Although, when I was a girl, my mom and I would spend most of our time baking. Every year before Christmas, we'd spend an entire weekend baking all sorts of goodies from cookies to caramel corn to pies of every flavor. Kaity even baked her first apple pie this year."

"That sounds like a perfect family tradition," he said, with a bit of melancholy in his voice.

"It is pretty perfect. Except for the fact that I'm usually working the extra pounds off my hips until St. Patrick's Day."

"I happen to like these hips just the way they are," he said, coming up behind me and placing his arms around my waist. I leaned back into him, enjoying the comfort of his embrace. "You know, I failed to get anything for dessert. Do you think you could come up with something," he whispered.

"Oh, I just need a few simple ingredients to make my specialty brownies. I can usually find them in most kitchens," I said, hopping off the stool. "As long as you have flour, eggs, sugar, and cocoa powder," I added, ticking the items off with my fingers.

"That wasn't exactly the dessert I was hoping for, but brownies do sound delicious. I should have all those ingredients in the pantry," he said, nodding his head.

"Great, I'll get started then," I said, looking for a mixing bowl.

As we prepared our dishes, we both had plenty of elbow room to cook in the large kitchen, but Blake used every opportunity to brush up against me.

"Excuse me," he said, pressing against my back as I stirred the brownie batter. "Do you need any help over here?"

"No, I think I got it," I smiled, turning toward him.

"I think I'll be the judge of that," he said, reaching behind me to stick his finger in the bowl.

"What—what do you think you're doing?" I asked, as he wiped the chocolate over my lips.

Instinctively, I began licking the chocolate from my lips. "Uh uh, that batter was for me," he said, guiding my lips toward his. I moaned as he cradled my face between his palms, not even caring that there was now chocolate all over the side of my face. Our tongues clashed together for what seemed like several minutes until I was nearly seeing stars. I wasn't sure if it was from lack of oxygen, or just from the effect that Blake was having on me.

His mouth still on mine, Blake picked me off the ground and gently placed me on the counter. Feeling his arousal hard on my belly, I wrapped my legs around his waist. Just as he began lifting the hem of my shirt, my nipples hardening from the closeness of his hands, the oven buzzed alerting us that dinner was ready.

"Fuck," Blake groaned, pulling his lips away from mine. "I guess I should take the potatoes out of the oven before they burn," he added, dropping the hem of my shirt.

Exhaling, I dropped my head back in frustration. "Yeah, I guess that's a good idea."

He chuckled, seemingly proud of his ability to leave me hot and bothered. "Why don't you go get washed up. I'll put the brownies in a pan and stick them in the oven. Dinner will be ready when you come out."

"Why do I have to clean up before dinner? What am I six now?" I laughed, forgetting my face was covered in brownie batter.

"The chocolate," he laughed, pointing at my face. "I may have gotten it all over your face."

"Oh, right," I said, smiling. "I'll be right back then," I added, hopping off the counter. I wasn't sure, but I thought I heard Blake let out a quiet groan as I walked toward the bathroom making sure to add a little sway to my step.

"I know what you're trying to do, Carpenter," he yelled.

"I have no idea what you're talking about, Mitchell," I sassed before shutting the door.

"SO, I WANTED to tell you this last night, but then things didn't go as planned," he said, opening a bottle of red wine to pair with the steaks.

"It's in the past, Blake. Don't even worry about it," I said, trying to reassure him. "What did you want to tell me?"

"Well, I've actually decided to move to D.C. Rich asked me to come and work with him since they've been short-staffed at the

Post since Brooke has been spending most of her time at their place in Michigan," Blake explained. "Besides, I think it would be a good move for me. It's an assistant editorship, and I don't see that in my future at the *Times* anytime soon."

I wasn't sure why, but for a moment I was disappointed that even though Blake would be moving, he wasn't really moving any closer to me.

"Rich also mentioned that they've been looking into adoption so that would take her away for even longer," he continued, not seeming to notice my lack of excitement for his new position.

"Wait! My best friend has been looking into adoption and she hasn't told me?" I screeched.

"Well, Rich started investigating it on his own, and didn't tell Brooke until just a few days ago. He didn't want to get her hopes up after all of their recent disappointment with the fertility treatments not working. I guess they have a meeting with a social worker in the next few days."

"I'm an awful friend," I sighed. "That would explain why she's called me so many times lately. I was just assuming she wanted to harass me about the trip so I've been sending her calls to voicemail."

"Well, knowing Brooke, I'm sure that was partially a reason for the calls, too," Blake laughed, trying to make me feel better for ignoring her calls.

"You're probably right. I guess I'll give her a call when I get back to the hotel later."

"Enough talk about our friends. I want to know more about Cass."

"OK," I said, squirming in the chair, suddenly feeling uncomfortable. "I'll do my best. What do you want to know?"

"Everything and anything. But I'll start easy on you, tell me about your family," Blake said, as he poured us a second glass of wine.

"Not much to tell really. My parents have been married for almost forty years. I'm an only child and still spoiled rotten," I admitted with a sly smile. "Brooke's dad and my dad were best friends in college, and that's how Brooke and I met. She's definitely my sister from another mister. We've pretty much been inseparable for as long as I can remember."

"I think that's awesome. I've never had a friendship like that," he said.

"No? What about Rich? I thought you two had been friends for a long time."

"No, not really. We've only been friends for just a few years. We met in grad school and I guess we just clicked right away. Don't get me wrong, I love him like a brother, but we just don't have the same kind of history as you and Brooke do."

"Oh, trust me, that's not always a good thing. She has more dirt on me than I care to admit," I laughed.

"Sounds like a story there," he said, raising his brow.

"Probably more than one, but I think those should be saved for another day," I suggested. "We've covered my family. Now it's your turn."

"Changing the subject, I see. OK, OK, I won't push my luck," he smirked.

"Smart man," I grinned.

"I'll remember you said that," he joked. "Anyways, my family . . . Mom and Dad have been married for forty-seven years now. I have an older brother, Kevin, who's actually a little over ten years older than me. My parents had him when they were both really young, and then after a series of miscarriages they'd decided to remain a family of three. Let's just say that I gave them the surprise of their lifetime."

"I love that," I beamed. "I'm sure they couldn't have been

happier with the news."

"Growing up, I was always the apple of my mother's eye," he said, reminiscing. "I loved it, but Kevin didn't appreciate it much–that's for sure."

"Sibling rivalry?" I asked.

"I think that's an understatement. We don't really talk to each other much–even now."

"Really?" I questioned, not really sure if I should press the conversation further.

"He's in California. He's divorced and has three kids. I haven't seen him since my wedding. He did call after Alyssa died, but it almost seemed like my mother forced him to do it," he said, shrugging. "I don't know. It is what it is, I suppose."

He paused for a moment as if lost in his own thoughts. "Do you want more kids," he asked, his question catching me by surprise.

"Is this where the questions get harder?" I asked.

"That wasn't my intent, Cass," he said, trying to reassure me. "Listen, you don't have to answer anything that makes you uncomfortable."

"No, it's OK," I paused, not really knowing how to answer his question. "Um, to be honest, I'm not exactly sure anymore."

"I don't understand," he said, shaking his head.

"Well, growing up, I always wanted a big family. My mom and dad have such a perfect marriage that I just assumed all relationships were that way. Hopeless romantic, remember?" I said with a nervous laugh. "Even though Brooke was like a sister, it wasn't quite the same. I always wanted that bond. I knew I wanted my kids to have that.

Then when Steve left me knocked up, everything changed. It's ironic because even though Steve gave me a child, he robbed me of my ability to have a family. At least the family I'd always envisioned for myself."

"You're wrong, Cass," Blake said, seriousness in his voice. "He didn't rob you of anything, you just forgot how to believe. If you'll let me, I want to help you remember how to believe again."

It may have been the delicious meal, or the lit candles flickering between us, but in that moment, I truly wanted to believe. "I'd like that, too," I whispered, nodding my head in agreement.

Chapter Thirteen

BLAKE

AFTER WE'D FINISHED dinner, Cass insisted on helping me clear the table and load the dishwasher. We continued into the living room, carrying the full pan of brownies for dessert. As I flicked the switch to the fireplace, Cass took a seat on the couch.

"Can I get you anything else? Another glass of wine, maybe?" I asked, as she pulled a blanket across her lap.

"Blake Mitchell, if I didn't know any better, I would assume you were trying to get me drunk," she tittered.

"Well, you can't blame a guy for trying. If I remember correctly, the last time you were drunk, you did a little striptease for me."

"Oh my god! I still can't believe I did that!" she admitted, a flush creeping up her face.

"Well I certainly enjoyed the show. Here's to hoping I get to see more next time," I teased, raising my glass of wine.

"Stop it!" she squealed, covering her face with the blanket.

"You stop it," I laughed, plucking a throw pillow off the couch and tossing it at her. "Since when has Cassidy Carpenter had a shy bone in her body?"

"I don't know," she confessed, lowering the blanket. "You just make me feel, I guess. It's not something I'm used to."

Suddenly our playful banter had taken a serious turn. Little by little, I was breaking down Cass's wall–revealing her vulnerability. Twisting the ring on my finger, I knew what I needed to do before this could go any further between us. My heart knew when I first saw Cass that this was something I needed to do, but it had taken longer for my head to catch up. If she was revealing herself to me, it was my turn to give her my all. It was time to say *goodbye*.

"I'll be right back. Make yourself comfortable," I said, retreating down the hallway to the bedroom.

Excusing myself, I needed to do this alone and in my own way. Opening the drawer to the nightstand, I removed the black velvet box which held Alyssa's diamond engagement ring and wedding band. Removing it from her finger just minutes before closing the casket had been one of the most difficult moments in my life. I only took it, thinking that someday Maddy might want it as a reminder of her mother.

Turning to Rich, he took Alyssa's ring from his pocket and placed it in my palm. Using the pad of my thumb, I swiped a fresh tear from my bride's cheek before continuing with my vows. "Alyssa, my beautiful, gorgeous bride, today I take you as my wife. From the moment I first laid my eyes on you in that coffee shop in the middle of downtown Manhattan, I knew I needed you in my life. From this day forward, I promise to love you without reservation, comfort you in times of sorrow, encourage you to achieve all of your goals, laugh with you and cry with you, always be open and honest with you, raise a family together with you, and grow old with you all while cherishing you for as long as we both shall live. Never goodbye," I vowed, sliding the ring on her finger.

"Blake, my handsome groom and best friend, today I take you as my husband. Together we'll create a home, joining our lives and our families. I vow to help create a life that we can cherish, inspiring your love for me and mine for you. I promise to be honest, caring, and truthful

to you as you are and not as I want you to be. We'll grow old together and love one another for as long as we both shall live. Never goodbye," she said, placing the tungsten band around my finger.

Thinking back on that moment, I truly believed then that it would never be goodbye and forever would last a lot longer than just a handful of years. Even after I was grazed in the shoulder by a stray bullet as Rich and I covered a political rally a few years back, I still thought we were invincible–living in our perfect little bubble.

"It's time to finally say goodbye, Lys. I've found someone, and she makes me happy. I think you'd like her a lot. She's Brooke's best friend, and she's great with our kids. You'll always be my first love, but I think it's time to open my heart to someone else. I can't do that while I'm still holding on to you–to this ring. Truth is, I think I'm already falling in love with her. I hope you understand," I said out loud as I slipped my wedding band off my finger, placing it in the velvet box. Looking at the rings together in the box, I exhaled sharply before snapping it closed. "Goodbye, Short Stack. I love you–I'll always love you."

Placing the box back in the nightstand, I sat on the edge of the bed for a moment before returning to the living room to talk to Cass. I needed a minute to think about what I'd just done. Raking my fingers through my hair, I wondered if I should even tell her how I was feeling. We'd had such a good conversation at dinner that I feared this might set her back again.

"Hey, you were gone a long time," she said as I walked back into the room, sitting beside her on the couch.

"Yeah, there was something I needed to do," I confessed, reaching for her hand.

As our hands locked together, she let out an audible gasp. "You took off your wedding ring?" she asked, cautiously.

"It was time. I want to move forward with you, and I couldn't properly do that while I was wearing another woman's ring," I said, hoping she could hear the sincerity in my tone. "I don't know what the future holds for us, Cass, but I want to find out. Take this leap with me?"

She stared at me for what seemed like an eternity before finally responding. "OK, let's try," she said.

"Yeah? We're doing this?" I questioned.

"Yes, we're doing this. Now shut up and kiss me, Mitchell."

"Now that's an order I can get behind," I growled, clutching the nape of her neck, bringing her lips to mine. As our lips touched, her hands became entangled in my hair, only deepening our kiss. As much as I didn't want to rush her into anything, I craved her–all of her.

Not wanting to disrespect Cass by taking her back into the bedroom, the same bedroom where I'd just said goodbye to Alyssa, I eyed the couch we were sitting on. Resting one knee beside her and placing my other foot on the ground, I gently lowered her back to the couch. I hovered over her, continuing my onslaught on her lips.

Stopping for a moment to catch my breath, I gazed down at her, taking sight of her chest as it rose and fell with her own rapid breaths.

"Cass, if you want me to stop, you need to tell me right now. Because once I start, I'm not sure if I'll be able to control myself," I warned, staring into her dilated pupils. She was as ravenous for me as I was for her.

"Don't stop," she said, barely above a whisper.

"Say it louder," I growled.

"Don't stop! I want you Blake–all of you," she said louder than before.

Those were the only words I needed to hear as I slid my hands under her shirt, unhooking her bra. Moving my hands to her front,

I grazed her full breasts causing her to squirm beneath my weight.

"As much as I want to take this slow, I don't know how much more time we have alone," I whispered.

"Then stop wasting time," she sassed, as she sat up and ripped her shirt and bra off in one quick movement.

As much time as we'd spent together in the last few weeks, Cass still kept me on my toes–always surprising me. Lying back, she grabbed my hand in hers, guiding me to her chest. Placing both of my hands on her breasts, she directed my palms as they slid across her already hardened nipples. Thinking her dominatrix side was pretty sexy, I decided to let Cass take control–for now.

"Just like this," she ordered, removing her hand from mine. "Don't stop." As I continued palming her breasts, tweaking and pinching her nipples, she reached her hands over and popped the button of my jeans before slowing working down the zipper, my already erect cock springing free from the waist of my boxer briefs. Circling her fingers around the head of my cock, I nearly lost it before it even really began.

"I think it's my turn to take the driver's seat," I growled. Pulling down her leggings, it left just the thin fabric of her panties between us.

"You're so goddamn beautiful," I growled, before placing a trail of heated kisses down her chest and stomach, stopping just above the waist of her panties. Knowing I didn't have much more time, I quickly stood and discarded my clothes, letting them drop to the floor.

Crawling back onto the couch, I rested my weight on one arm as I took the other hand and slowly slid Cass's panties over, exposing her pretty, pink pussy. She moaned beneath me as I stroked my thumb over her already wet core. The expressions on her face as I inserted one finger and then another, left me wanting to jizz all over her stomach without even properly fucking her.

"Faster, Blake. Faster," she moaned as I inserted a third finger into her already pulsating center. Waiting until just the right moment, I used my thumb to stroke her clit causing an orgasm to ripple over her body. If her orgasm felt that good around my fingers, I could only imagine what it would feel like with my cock buried deep inside her pussy.

As she lay there, trying to catch her breath, I reached for my pants which I'd tossed on the floor. Pulling out the condom which I'd grabbed earlier, Cass sat and stared at me with a sleepy smile forming across her lips.

"Let me," she said through hooded eyes. Allowing her to take the condom, I leaned back, resting my weight on my ankles. My fully erect cock standing at full attention, just waiting for her to touch it. Ripping open the package, she placed the condom at my tip before slowly sheathing it in its entirety.

Exhaling deeply, I sat back on my knees, lining up my dick with her entrance. Drawing her into me, I feverishly kissed her before sinking into her pussy as we both dropped back onto the couch. I pumped into her, the sound of my balls smacking against her ass, as I dug my fingers into the flesh of her back. Rocking my hips back and forth, I continued to fill her to the hilt with each thrust. Her breathing became ragged and I knew she was close to her release.

"Not yet, Cass. Stay with me a little longer," I said, slowing my motion.

"Please, don't stop. I need to come, Blake. Please let me come."

"Fuck! You're so fucking hot right now. You, naked beneath me while you scream my name, have got to be the hottest, fucking thing I've ever seen," I growled, pounding into her once more.

"Are you ready to come, Carpenter?" I asked.

"Mmmhmm," she moaned, arching her back, her nipples standing at full attention.

"Louder!" I yelled, tweaking her right nipple with my finger as I bit down on the left.

"Fuck!" she yelped.

"I'll take that as a yes," I smirked. "We're going to do this together. You understand?"

Nodding her head, I stroked her clit with my thumb as I slammed into her pussy once more, sending her over the edge. Rocking my hips back and forth once more, I came undone with my own orgasm. Taking a few breaths to try and calm my beating heart, I rolled onto my side as to not crush Cass beneath my weight.

"That was—."

"Amazing," I interrupted her, not allowing her to finish her thought.

"I was going to say fucking amazing, but just amazing works, too," she giggled.

"No, you're right. That was fucking amazing," I agreed.

We lay in silence for several minutes, before I felt Cass's hands on my chest and shoulders. Tracing my scar with her finger, I knew I owed her an explanation.

"That's where I was hit by a stray bullet," I said, the haunting memory replaying in my mind. "I'm sure Brooke told you all about it."

"Yeah," she said. "She thought Rich died that day. Luckily you were both all right," she added, resting her head against my chest as I told her the rest of the story.

"He may have saved my life. I was only grazed on the shoulder by the bullet, but I did lose a lot of blood. If Rich hadn't stepped in like he did, I'm not sure how things would've turned out.

"You'd think that my near-death experience would've prepared me for when we lost Alyssa, but it didn't at all. In fact, I think it only made me think we were even more invincible than I already believed we were."

We lay there talking for a few more minutes before hearing a commotion out in the hallway to the apartment. Cass sat straight up, wrapping her arms around her chest.

"Please tell me your parents don't have a key," she squealed, her eyes wide as saucers.

"Yes! They do," I yelled. "Hurry, get up! I'll grab the clothes!" Picking the clothes off the floor, I threw them at her in the bathroom before hurrying into the bedroom. Slipping into a pair of sweatpants that I'd worn the night before, I threw a T-shirt on over my head before running back out into the living room just in time for the front door to open.

"We knocked, but you didn't answer," my mother said as the kids ran past her.

"Yeah, we were just cleaning up after dinner," I said, hoping my mother believed my lie. Yes, I was a grown ass man lying to his mother. I'm not proud, but sometimes it had to be done.

"Where's my mommy?" Kaity asked, staring up at me.

"I'm right here, Princess," Cass responded, stepping out into the living room. Biting my tongue, I nearly lost it when I noticed her clothes.

Trying to get Cass's attention, I failed as Kaity enthusiastically started telling us about their evening.

"Mommy, I had so much fun with my new Geema and Geepa. We saw a movie, and ate lots and lots of popcorn."

"That's great, Baby. I'm glad you had so much fun."

"Mommy?" Kaity said, her expression changing as she finally looked up at her mother.

"Yeah, Baby?"

"Why is your shirt on backwards?"

Looking down, Cass's forehead creased and a look mixed with shame and guilt flashed across her face. "I, uh," she stuttered, realizing that my parents were also in the room.

Knowing I needed to step in and do something before Cass fled my apartment, I interrupted before she was able to finish her thought. "She spilled food on her shirt when we were eating dinner. She went into the bathroom to wash the stain out. She must've accidently put it on backwards when she slipped it back on. Right, Cass?" I said, nodding my head, hoping she'd agree with me.

"Yep, silly me! I'm so embarrassed," she said, her cheeks flushing.

"Don't be embarrassed, Darling. It's happened to us all," my mom said.

"Thank you. You must be Mrs. Mitchell. Blake has told me so much about you," Cass said.

"Don't believe anything my son has told you about us," Mom chuckled. "And, please, call me Penny. And, this is Blake's father Dennis," she added, as the girls ran off to the bedroom to play. As Kaity ran by Cass, I was almost certain that little girl was going to get an earful later for embarrassing her mother.

"It's a pleasure to meet you both," Cass said, forcing a smile. We exchanged in a few minutes of brief conversation before my parents excused themselves and exited, after telling us of an impending snowstorm.

"Well that was probably the most awkward experience of my life," Cass said after my parents had left. "I'm sure they think super highly of the girl who just walked out of their son's bathroom with sex-crazed hair, swollen lips, and a backwards T-shirt. But, thanks for just telling them that I have no hand-eye coordination because that was so much less embarrassing," she added, covering her face with her hands.

"It's official, I can never see them again," she sighed.

"Would you stop it. We're adults, Cass. They're adults. They know what adults do," I tried reassuring her.

"Fine, if you say so," she sighed.

"I do. Just trust me?" I asked, tucking a loose strand of hair behind her ear.

"I do," she said with a faint smile. "And, as much as I don't want to leave, we should probably get going too."

"Stay the night?" I asked. In my head, I knew it was probably too soon, but I didn't want her to leave especially when she was flying home the next day.

"I don't think that's a good idea, Blake. I don't want Kaity to get the wrong idea," she explained, her forehead creasing again. "Besides, I didn't bring anything extra with me. We don't have a change of clothes, or even our toothbrushes."

"I'm sure Maddy has something big enough that Kaity can wear, and I think you'd be pretty fucking sexy wearing a pair of my sweats and a button-down shirt," I groaned. "Please, say you'll stay. I probably even have an extra toothbrush or two. Besides, I really don't want you out there riding around in an Uber when the roads are bad."

She chewed on her bottom lip for a moment before answering, "Fine, but I'm sleeping with Kaity in your spare bedroom."

"But," I tried arguing.

"No, buts, Mitchell," she said, waving her finger at me.

"Are you sure I can't get you to change your mind? Something tells me that Round Two will be even more fucking amazing than Round One, Carpenter," I said with a wink.

"Ugh, you don't play fair!" she yelled, swatting my arm.

"I never said I did, Babe."

Chapter Fourteen

CASSIDY

*W*AKING UP IN the morning, wrapped in Blake's strong arms, wasn't something in my game plan. My head was telling me that everything between us was moving too fast, but Blake asked me to believe so that's what I was trying to do.

After spending the night together, in Blake's spare bedroom, saying goodbye as he dropped us off in front of the terminal was a lot more difficult than I'd ever expected it to be. We hadn't made specific plans to see each other again as the details of his upcoming move to D.C. were still up in the air, but Blake promised that it wouldn't be long, saying that he would visit as soon as he and the kids had settled into their new environment.

Walking from the gate, after arriving back in Michigan, lost in a memory of Blake's lips locked onto mine, I nearly ran smack dab into Brooke who was waiting for us at the baggage claim area. I'd told her several times before we left that I could just leave my car in the long-term parking, but she insisted on handling our transportation to and from the airport.

"Aunt Brookie! I missed you!" Kaity squealed, running into Brooke's outstretched arms.

"Hi there, Princess! I missed you, too," she said, squeezing my daughter so tight that I thought she might pop. "Tell me all about your trip! Don't leave out anything!"

"Well, let's see," Kaity said, looking up toward the ceiling, probably deciding on which story to tell Brooke first. "Oh, I know, I have a new Geema and Geepa!" she said, excitement in her voice.

With this new bit of information, Brooke eyed me suspiciously. "You do?" she asked, hoping to pry more information from my daughter. We'd been friends far too long. It was time for me to turn the tables.

"She's just talking about some people who I met for work. It was an older husband and wife team who run this particular bridal boutique, that's all. She really took a liking to them. Norma and Dean–they were really sweet," I said, hoping she'd buy my story.

"Norma and Dean, huh? I could've sworn you told me on the phone that you met with a group of women?" she questioned.

"Did I? I think you must've misunderstood me," I said, burying myself further into the lie.

"Mommy," Kaity said, tugging on the hem of my coat. "I thought Geema and Geepa said they were Penny and Dennis?"

"Penny and Dennis, huh?" Brooke said, twisting the corner of her mouth. "I've met Blake's parents before. Really nice people."

Knowing I'd been caught in a lie, I leaned my head back in frustration before my daughter unknowingly continued to dig my hole.

"Aunt Brookie, look what else!" Kaity beamed, rummaging through her bag, pulling out her new doll. "Look what Blake bought me in the Apple!"

"Wow! That's a pretty nice present, Kaity. And, I think you mean the Big Apple," Brooke said, her mouth turning into a smile.

"Oh yeah, why do they call it the Big Apple? Maybe they should call it the Big Banana instead. Bananas taste way better than apples," she said innocently, as we both chuckled at her naivety.

"She's not even five and she already loves the banana. I'm in big trouble," I said as we both laughed.

"So, Cass, enough with the stories, when were you going to tell me that you saw Blake?"

"I didn't want to tell you because I knew you'd make a bigger deal out of it than it was," I lied, my eyes darting back and forth. If Brooke really knew the truth about Blake and me, she'd die because I hadn't told her sooner. I knew that it was probably best to come clean now rather than dig myself into an even deeper hole, but I wanted to keep our relationship between the two of us to myself for just a bit longer. I was just hoping that my chatterbox daughter wouldn't spill the beans before I was ready.

"You're so full of shit!" Brooke exclaimed.

"Mommy, Aunt Brookie said a bad word," Kaity squealed.

"Sorry, Princess. I should've said that your mommy was full of poop," she said, correcting herself.

"It's OK," Kaity said, reaching for her tiny, purple suitcase as it came down the conveyor belt.

"Seriously, Brooke. We just had lunch. That's all–it was nothing."

"Yeah, you're still lying to me. You're doing that thing you always do with your eyes."

"OK, he invited me over for dinner, too," I confessed, already revealing more than I cared to.

"Did you kiss him?" she asked, obviously not letting this go.

"I'm done talking about this, Brooke. Let it go. Please," I nearly begged.

"You so kissed him!" she squealed. "Oh my god, did you two have sex?" she questioned, whispering the last word.

"I said drop it!" I nearly yelled, causing a few people around us to turn in our direction.

"Fine, I will, but only because we're in the middle of an air-port. But, once we're back in the car, you're spilling it! All.of.it." she said.

I sighed, knowing that this was a battle I was bound to lose. Collecting our luggage, we walked out into the short-term parking area, the frosty January air nearly taking my breath away. After loading our bags into the trunk and fastening Kaity into her booster seat, I slid into the passenger seat.

"Spill it," Brooke said, turning to me before pulling out into traffic.

"OK, but you're not going to be very happy with me," I con-fessed.

"Well, I'm already not very happy with you. So, you might as well tell me everything."

"Fine, Blake paid for our trip to New York. We took the kids sledding while he was here over Christmas, and he wanted to see me again. So, he came over on Christmas, and gave me the plane tickets.

"At first, I told him I couldn't accept them, but he eventually wore me down. I've learned that he's pretty good at that," I said, smiling at his ability at doing that the night before, as he argued with me about spending the night together in the same bed.

Understanding that it wouldn't be right for us to sleep in the same bed as he shared with Alyssa, he told Kaity that she could sleep in a king-sized bed all by herself. Kaity loved the idea, and begged me until I relented.

"Yep, you're right. I'm definitely not very happy with you for keeping this from me! I thought we told each other everything, Cass!" she yelled.

"Can we go sledding again Mommy?" Kaity piped in from the back seat.

"Kaity, can you please put your headphones on so your Aunt

Brooke and I can have an adult conversation, please?" I asked.

"But, I want to talk, too, Mommy!" she pouted.

"We'll talk when we get home. Please do this for this time, OK?" I asked again.

"Fine," she huffed, rummaging through her bag.

"Anyways, where were we?" I asked Brooke.

"I was telling you how much of a pain in the ass you were for not telling me about your love affair with my husband's best friend," she yelled, giving me the classic stink-eye.

"You're being dramatic, and it's hardly a love affair. Besides, it all just happened so fast. I didn't mean for any of it to happen." I said, leaning my head back in frustration.

"Wait, did this all start at my wedding? Has this been going on for months?" she asked.

"No!" I nearly screamed. "I promise it hasn't been going on that long. He did ask me out at your wedding, but I told him no. I didn't want to date and I told him that. Honestly, I still don't know if I want to date. I'm so confused!"

"Are you two dating then?" she asked.

"Yeah, kinda. I told him I would try," I said, shrugging. "It just sucks that he's so far away."

"Yeah, did he tell you that he was moving to D.C.?" Brooke asked.

"Yeah, he did. I also had to hear from him that my best friend might be adopting a baby!"

"I tried calling you, but you were avoiding me. I thought I'd done something to piss you off, but I now see that isn't the case," Brooke remarked, slyly.

"I'm sorry. I should've answered. If I'd had any idea that you were thinking about adoption then you know I would've answered. I want to hear all about it."

"I don't know much yet," she said, biting down on her bottom lip–a nervous trait she'd done since we were kids. "We're meeting with a social worker, who Rich knows, next week. I just want to be a mom, Cass. I can't take this constant rejection month after month. It's killing me, and Rich has been a mess, too."

"I know, Brookie. But, you two are good, right? Don't tell me that I have to kick Dick in the ass," I said with a half-smile.

"No, he's been great. I definitely wouldn't be able to do this without him," she said. "And, don't think I didn't notice you going and trying to change the subject on me. I still want to know more about you and Blake."

"I've told you everything," I said, knowing that I left out the little detail that we'd had sex.

"Everything?" she questioned, raising her brow.

"Yes, everything," I lied again.

"You never did answer me when I asked you if you'd had s-e-x," she said.

I stared at her, hoping against hope that she'd just drop it, but no such luck. "Well?" she asked again.

"Fine, we did. Twice actually. And, it was effing amazing. Probably the best I've ever had," I confessed, her eyes practically popping out of her head at my candidness. "You happy now?"

"Holy shit! You and Blake, huh. You two are going to get married and have babies and live happily-ever-after just like you always dreamed about," Brooke fantasized.

"You're such a hopeless romantic. You know I don't believe in that stuff anymore. This is probably nothing more than a fling. I mean he lives practically five-hundred miles away," I sighed, wishing for a minute that Brooke's dream for me was really a possibility.

"Mommy, if you're having a baby does that mean I'll be a big sister?" Kaity interrupted from the back seat.

I stared at Brooke a minute, trying to contain my laughter,

before turning to answer my daughter, "Kaitlyn Olivia Carpenter, I thought I told you to put your headphones on?"

"But, I wanted to listen!" she cried.

"Headphones, now!" I yelled, as Brooke pulled into the driveway.

"Should I tell Kaity that since we're home now, it probably doesn't matter if she has her headphones on?" Brooke laughed.

After helping us unload our luggage, Brooke left saying she had some business to attend to before their meeting with the social worker next week. Even though she said we were good, I suspected she was still a little upset with me.

We'd been home for just a few minutes, when my phone dinged with an incoming text. I smiled seeing Blake's name flash across my screen.

> *Blake: I heard you made it home safely. You could've given me a heads-up that you were going to let Brooke in on our little arrangement.*

That little bitch had already blabbed everything to Rich. I shouldn't be surprised, she'd always been horrible at keeping secrets. I was going to let her have it when I saw her next time.

> *Cass: Sorry, she knew something was going on the minute I stepped off the plane. I didn't stand a chance, especially when she started using Kaity to her advantage. That little lady is trouble with a capital T. I take it Rich let you have it, too?*

> *Blake: Yep, he called to give me shit. I mean we're dudes so we don't really get worked up about secrets and shit, but it still would've been nice to know it was coming. You know so we could get our stories straight.*

Cass: Sorry, she must've literally told him the second after she dropped us off. I was going to call you in just a few minutes, I promise.

Blake: It's fine, Carpenter. I'm not really upset. ;) And, as much as I'd love to hear your sexy-as-fuck voice, I'm actually about to leave on an assignment. I'll call you later tonight?

Cass: I'll be waiting, Mitchell. Oh, and, thanks for this weekend. We really did have a great time.

Blake: You're welcome, Beautiful. I'll talk to you later.

Cass: TTYL.

Chapter Fifteen

CASSIDY

NEARLY A MONTH had passed since I'd last seen Blake in New York, and what a whirlwind of activity it had been since that time. Just a week after Rich and Brooke had met with their social worker, she'd asked them to consider fostering a three-year-old boy. The child's mother had been killed in a car accident when he was just seven months old, and his father's name wasn't even listed on his birth certificate.

The boy's mother had also been orphaned which left him without any known family members. He'd been in the care of a young couple for the last year. However, the husband received word of an out-of-town job transfer, and the two were expecting a child of their own. With the move, they were unable to take Brendan with them.

Because Rich had already started the fostering process weeks earlier, they were able to take Brendan into their home almost immediately. Knowing they wanted Brendan as a permanent part of their family, they'd already begun the formal adoption process. In just a few months, my best friend would finally be the mother that she so desperately wanted to be.

Also during the month, Blake had moved his family from New

York to begin his position at the *Post*. I still secretly wished he'd been able to move closer to me, but I understood that this was in everyone's best interest–except for mine.

Even though we Facetimed nearly every night, it wasn't the same as having Blake with me in person. It was funny how I'd gone about life as a strong, independent woman for the last several years without as much as even thinking about a man in my life. Now, I couldn't even reach something on the top shelf at the grocery store without thinking about how much easier it would be if Blake were with me.

And, I won't even mention my increased sexual appetite since Blake had made me come not once, but three times that night. All I could think about since I left the Big Apple was my pussy riding Blake's Big Cock. And, it was those very same fantasies to begin with that lead me to my most recent health crisis, if you could call it that.

I was blaming it all on the damn vibrator. My mother had been right all those years before. "Those damn things are nothing but trouble," she'd say. I could hear her now, "You're going straight to hell if you use one of those devil toys."

I may not be going to hell, but I couldn't walk either–all because I'd tripped over the fucking vibe. Now, I needed to seek medical attention as my ankle was already what could be called a cankle and was turning the deep purple color of an eggplant.

Writhing on the bedroom floor, I screamed out in pain hoping someone would hear me. Glancing at my window, I cringed remembering I'd closed it before embarking on my latest sexual escapade. I hadn't wanted Fay, my much-too-nosey, elderly neighbor, hearing me climax. Now, I felt as though I might pass out, or worse, die on the bedroom floor. No one would even come to my rescue, if my screams couldn't be heard. Instead, I was left hoping that the life insurance policy I'd taken out had a vibrator clause.

Crawling across the floor to reach the phone, I noticed Kaity standing in the doorway. My little angel–sent from heaven above to come rescue her mother! Little did I know then that she'd actually turn out to be my little devil in disguise.

"Kaity, can you please bring Mommy her phone? I need to call Aunt Brookie," I asked.

"Are you OK, Mommy? I'm scared," she confessed, tears streaming down her cheeks.

Of course, I'm the one who wanted to cry, yet had to remain the calm, cool and collected one in order to ease her nerves. Damn you Brooke for rubbing your emotional side off on my daughter. You'd really think genetics would win out. Thanks for that, biology.

"I'll be fine, Baby. I just need to call Auntie Brooke so she can take me to the doctor. Mommy has a big owie on her foot."

"Oh, I'll kiss it and make the owie go away like you always do for me!" she said, seemingly pleased with herself for thinking of such a cure.

"I'd love a kiss, Kaity, but I really think I need a doctor for this one. You remember, like the time a while back when your ear hurt so bad that even Mommy's kisses couldn't make it better?"

"Oh, I do remember. That's the time we had to go to the big doctor's office late at night. They gave me a grape sucker before we left there, right?" she said, rubbing her chin.

Jesus, sometimes my child just talked too damn much. In the time it took her to get me the damn phone, I could've limped my way to the emergency room.

"Yes, Baby, that's right. Now can you please hand Mommy the phone?" I sighed.

Finally, with the phone in hand, I dialed Brooke. Luckily, she picked up on the first ring.

"Brooke, can you drive me to the ER? I think I broke my

ankle," I screeched.

"What? How'd you do that?" she asked.

"It's not important. Just please hurry. It's already been too long. At this rate, my bones will have fused back together and they'll have to break them again at the hospital before inserting a titanium rod and six screws."

"OK, drama queen. I'll be there as soon as I can, but first I need to see if Rich can come home to stay with Brendan."

"No! There's no time! I may lose my foot!"

"Oh my god. You're ridiculous. I'm on my way."

AFTER WAITING FOR what seemed like an eternity, a nurse finally called us back to an examining room. First she took my weight, which I totally didn't think was necessary for this type of injury, and then my vitals after which we were stuck waiting again. With two adults and two children crammed into the tiny room, the walls were beginning to close in on me. If the doctor didn't hurry, I'd be needing more than medical attention for my ankle.

"Seriously, if this doctor doesn't hurry, I'm going to need mouth-to-mouth."

"That can be arranged," I heard a deep male voice respond.

Looking up, I suddenly forgot why I was at the hospital to begin with. The man was a vision in light green scrubs and white coat. Perfectly styled hair, bronze skin, glistening teeth, and a stethoscope neatly hanging around his thick neck. I immediately felt my lady bits tingle in the presence of Dr. Adonis.

"Blake," Brooke coughed.

Glaring at her, I quickly turned my attention back to the doctor. After all, yes, I was committed to Blake, but that didn't mean I was dead, or couldn't window-shop. Besides, Blake lived in D.C. and since he'd just moved there he obviously didn't have any intention of leaving anytime soon. And, it could be argued that it was because of Blake that I was sitting in the ER to begin with. But, that would remain my little secret.

"What'd you say, Doctor?" I asked, secretly hoping this was a dream and that he'd revive me with his lips.

"Oh, I'm sorry, Miss . . ." he said, looking down at my chart. "Miss Carpenter. I was talking to my nurse out in the hallway– that must've been what you overheard. What seems to be the problem today? Your chart here mentions your ankle?" he said, coming over to check my pulse.

"Yeah, I tripped and twisted my ankle. It's turned a nasty shade of purple. I think it may be broken," I sighed, trying to avoid the entire story.

"Mmmhmm," he said, placing the stethoscope to my chest. "Please take a deep breath. OK, now exhale slowly."

"Something wrong?" I asked, unsure as to why he was listening to my chest when I'd come in worried about my tibia.

"Just standard procedure," he said. "When I came in the room, your pulse was racing so I just wanted to check things out."

I blushed, hoping he wouldn't realize it was the effect he was having on me. "Oh, I guess I'm just worried about what could be wrong?" I explained.

"OK, let's take a look then," he said, taking a seat on the rolling stool in front of the exam table.

"Of course," I answered, rolling up my pant leg. I tried making it look sexy until I saw unshaved legs and my purple ankle that was now the size of a watermelon. Nothing could possibly make that look sexy.

"I don't think anything is broken, but I do think you have a pretty severe sprain here. I'd like to take an X-ray, though, just to be sure," he said, as he began manipulating my foot. "What exactly happened? How'd you trip?"

I grimaced more from the embarrassment that I was facing than from the pain I felt from the doctor twisting my ankle.

"A Barbie," I blurted out. "It was dark in my room, and I tripped on one of my daughter's dolls. It rolled beneath my foot, and I twisted my ankle. I think my full body weight landed on it when I hit the floor." It was close enough to the truth, I thought.

Before the doctor even had a chance to respond, Kaitlyn interjected. Why did I bring her along? "Mommy! That's not true! My dolls were all put away. Just like you asked," she beamed, proudly.

"Kaity, it's fine, Baby. You must've forgotten one. I'm not mad," I tried reassuring her, hoping she would accept my story.

Much to my chagrin, she opted for the truth instead. Why'd I ever teach my daughter that lying was always wrong? "No, Mommy! It was that pink toy that you have. The one that you always say is 'Mommy's toy and I can't ever touch.' You know, the one you and Aunt Brookie named Bob," she said, innocently.

I could feel heat rising from my chest as Brooke broke into hysterical laughter.

"Oh my god, I need to go. My ankle is suddenly feeling just fine," I said, hopping off the table. The universe must've been playing tricks on me that day because my ankle gave out as I fell into the doctor's lap, my face mere inches away from his junk.

"Seriously! Could this day get any fucking worse?" I yelled, quickly trying to hop back up onto the table.

"Mommy said a bad word!" Kaity shouted. Even the doctor who'd been able to maintain professional composure during my daughter's story, couldn't contain his laughter any longer. His head thrown back, he let out a belly-laugh.

"Hey Cass, look on the bright side. At least it wasn't death by dicking," Brooke blurted out.

That did me in. I was utterly humiliated, but even I could see the humor in the entire situation. I leaned back onto the table and joined them in a chorus of laughter.

I'D BEEN HOME for a few hours, and just as the doctor had suspected, the X-rays revealed a Grade Two sprain. Providing me with instructions to keep my ankle iced, wrapped, and elevated, he'd also sent me home with crutches as I was not to put weight on the ankle for at least two weeks. If I followed instructions, my injury was expected to heal within four to six weeks. Since wedding season wasn't quite here, it wouldn't interfere much with my work schedule.

I suppose, all-in-all, it could've turned out much worse. The doctor even told us, as we were leaving, that I'd been his most entertaining patient he'd seen in a while. At first, I wasn't sure how I should take that comment–as a compliment or not, but then he discreetly handed me his cell number along with a prescription for mild pain killers.

Half-watching a rerun of Married . . . with Children, I held the number, which was scrawled on a prescription slip, between my fingers. I wasn't really sure what to do with it. I hadn't even told Brooke that he'd given it to me. After everything that I'd been through, the last thing I wanted was a lecture from my best friend. I couldn't blame her, she was Blake's friend, too. And, with everything that he'd recently endured, he definitely deserved better from me.

My phone rang beside me. Looking down, I saw Blake's name flash across the dimly lit screen. I quickly crumpled up the paper and hurled it across the room. In hindsight, I was acting ridiculously; It's not like he could've seen the number from his apartment in D.C.

"Hey, Blake. What's up?" I asked, casually.

"Carpenter, you don't have to play coy. I talked to Rich earlier.

He told me what happened with you today."

"He did?" I asked, hesitantly. How did Rich know that the doctor had given me his number? Had Brooke seen him slip it to me, after all? Oh god, he's probably golfing buddies with Rich. Fucking Dick Davis knows everyone. Here I'd just realized that Blake was it for me, and Rich went and ruined everything. "I can explain."

"There's nothing to explain, Cass," he said, not sounding upset. Maybe he didn't even care. Maybe me–our relationship–meant nothing to him.

"Oh," was all I managed to say before I started crying. Why the fuck was I crying? Brooke must've rubbed off on me. Her constant tears drove me crazy, and now here I was bawling like a baby.

"Why are you crying? Are you in pain? Maybe you should go back to the ER. I can call Rich and he can drive you. Or, maybe I should just call 9–1–1. Fuck, I just need to be there with you," he said, frantically.

I stopped, realizing I wasn't sure I'd heard him correctly. "Blake, stop. What did you say?"

"I need to be there with you. I should've been the one to take you to the hospital today. Brooke could've stayed with Kaity and then maybe the doctor wouldn't have learned the truth behind your injury." He sounded serious, but I knew he was smirking on the other end.

I took a deep breath, realizing he called because he'd heard about my injury and not because he thought I might be considering calling the sexy-as-hell doctor for a personal house call.

"Are you making fun of me, Mitchell?" I asked. "That vibe wouldn't even have been a problem if you were here!"

"You'll throw them all away when I get there then?" he asked, taunting me.

"Well, don't go acting crazy now! After all, we might want to play with them together." I sure hope he bought that reasoning because the thought of getting rid of every vibrator was heartbreaking. We'd had some great times together throughout the years.

He moaned before responding, "Now THAT I could get on board with. But that's the only time you're allowed to use them. I'll take care of you the rest of the time. Deal?"

It sounded fair enough. I'd get him to agree to other uses later. "Deal," I agreed. "Now, when will you be here?"

"Well, it was supposed to be a surprise, but I'll be there the day after tomorrow," he said. Opening the calendar on my phone, I realized the day after tomorrow was February fourteenth–Valentine's Day.

"You're coming on Valentine's Day?" I asked.

"Yes, and if things go according to plan then I won't be the only one coming on Valentine's Day," he chuckled.

"You're never going to stop, are you?" I giggled.

"No, I'm never going to stop flirting with you," he said matter-of-factly. "I guess you'll just have to live with it."

"Yes, Sir," I laughed.

"It's good to hear you laugh. You sounded so serious when I first called. Is something else bothering you?" he asked.

"No, I'm good," I said. "I just miss you. I'm glad you called though. You've made me feel better–about everything," I admitted.

"Anything for you, Cass. Now go get some rest, and I'll see you soon," he said.

"OK, have a good night."

"Night. Sweet dreams," he said before ending the call.

Sitting on the couch for a minute, I contemplated trying to use the crutches before deciding to just sleep on the sofa for the night.

I pulled a blanket around me and thought about everything Blake had told me. Before I had a chance to second-guess things, like I always had in the past, I let sleep consume me. *Maybe it was the drugs I'd taken earlier to numb the pain, or maybe it was just the comfort that Blake provided me. Could I actually be falling in love with him?*

Chapter Sixteen

CASSIDY

*A*FTER SPENDING THE last two days cooped up with Nurse Kaitlyn attached to my hip, I was craving some adult interaction. My daughter was a fine, little helper, but her constant chatter was beginning to drive me nuts. Brooke had planned on stopping by the day before, but had an unexpected visit from Brendan's caseworker. Everything had turned out fine; They'd even been given a date for the adoption hearing, but Brooke was too anxious to come over for a visit afterwards.

Glancing at my watch, I sighed knowing Blake's flight wouldn't be landing for another five hours. Even though Rich was technically Blake's new boss, he didn't want to press his luck by asking for time off when he'd only been at the *Post* for a few weeks. I understood his reasoning, but I still wished he could've come earlier. Valentine's Day would practically be over by the time he arrived in Michigan.

Looking down, I realized I should probably stop moping around and change out of my pajamas to get ready for Blake's arrival. Since my recent injury, I hadn't left the house and had neglected my personal appearance–including shaving my most sensitive areas–something I dared not neglect.

Just as I was preparing myself for the pain of standing, there came a light rapping on the door. Biting my lip to dull the pain of my ankle, I hopped up with the use of my crutches and hobbled to the door. Opening it, I was surprised to see that it was Blake standing outside.

"Blake! I didn't expect you so early! I'm a mess," I said, trying to block myself with the door.

"Don't be silly, Carpenter. You look as beautiful as ever, and these are for you," he said, holding out a bouquet of long-stemmed red roses along with a wrapped box.

"They're gorgeous, but you're going to have to set them on the counter for me. "I'm a little incapacitated here," I said, pointing toward my bandaged ankle. "Where are the kids?

"Brooke wanted to take them back to their place so they could meet Brendan. They're going to drop them off later," he explained.

"Sounds good to me. What's in the box?"

"Just a little something I picked out for us," he said, winking.

"Oh yeah, should I put on a movie for Kaity in her room?" I asked, wiggling my brow.

"That's probably not necessary, it's only a box of chocolates. But, now that you mention it, I am dying to get my hands on you," he admitted.

Kaity must've heard the mention of her name as she immediately came barreling out of her bedroom.

"Mommy, you lied to me! You said Blake wouldn't be here until after dinnertime," she yelled. "We just finished lunch!"

Blake chuckled at my daughter's ability to always catch me in a lie. "Your mommy didn't lie, Kaity. I did," he confessed.

"You did?" she asked, her eyes widening at his admission. "Lying is bad, Blake!"

"I know, Princess, but I really wanted to surprise your mommy.

It's a special day for couples, like your mommy and me, and I wanted to do something nice for her. Now, can you do me a favor and go back to your bedroom and play for a while?"

"Sure, Blake! Anything for you!" she beamed, looking up at him with stars in her eyes.

"Something tells me that I'm not the only Carpenter girl who has a crush on you, Mitchell," I said, as we heard the door to the bedroom close. "My daughter seems pretty smitten."

"Well, I think she's pretty great, too. I hope it was OK that I told her we were a couple? It kind of slipped before I'd realized what I'd said," he said, worry on his face.

"It's fine, Blake. I told you that I'd try, and that's exactly what we're doing. So, yes, everyone can know that we're a couple–including my daughter."

"Perfect," he said, a smile forming across his lips. "And, right now, I want to focus all my attention on that little girl's mommy," he said, placing a slow, lingering kiss on my lips. "I've been waiting to do that for weeks."

"Then why'd you stop?" I asked through hooded eyes.

"Because your daughter is right around the corner," he laughed, giving me another peck on the lips. "But, don't you worry, I definitely have plans for more later on." Just the mention of his plans for later left me tingling in all the right places.

"Now, weren't there doctor's orders to stay off that foot?" he asked, pointing to my injury.

"Yes, but I think I'd rather play doctor with you," I flirted, thinking Blake was even hotter than my Dr. Adonis from earlier in the week.

"Well then, screw later, I think I should properly examine you now. Make sure you've been following orders," he said, desire thick in his voice.

"But, I thought you were worried about Kaity," I said,

reminding him that we weren't alone.

"On second thought, she'll be fine. After all, when Rich and Brooke drop Maddy and Ben off then we'll have even more children here. Besides, there's a lovely little thing called a door lock," he whispered in my ear, as he scooped me off my feet and into his arms.

Peppering kisses across my neck, Blake carried me into the bedroom and splayed me across the bed, being careful not to jar my ankle. Sitting up, I rested myself on my elbows and watched Blake as he walked back across the room, making sure the door was locked.

"I've missed you," he said, lust glowing in his dark eyes. "I've missed your sexy, bedroom eyes, your sassy, little mouth and your plump lips," he said, drawing my lips to his before pulling away.

"Blake," I moaned.

"Not this time, Cass. This time I'm taking control," he growled. "Now, where was I?" he asked, nearly burning a hole through me with his steady gaze. "I've missed your ample tits as they bounce up and down while I'm fucking you," he said, ripping my camisole and bra over my head in a single motion.

"Holy fuck, that was hot," I moaned for what was yet to come. Lying back on the bed, he crawled on top of me, tracing circles around my left nipple with his tongue while pinching the right one with the tips of his fingers.

"But you know what I missed most of all?" he whispered in my ear, sending a chill up my spine.

I lay in silence for a moment, not realizing Blake had even asked me a question. "Did you not hear me, Cass?"

"I'm sorry, what?" I squeaked.

"Do you know what I missed most of all?" he asked again in a gravelly voice.

"Oh, um, no?" I panted, feeling my arousal intensify within

my core.

"I've missed the sight of your pink, wet pussy as it's spread open wide and waiting for me to fuck it," he hissed, reaching for the drawstring of my pajama bottoms. My jaw dropped and my back arched at Blake's words. Admittedly, if only to myself, I was falling for the sweet and swoony Blake, but this dirty-talking version was hot as fuck.

Blake stood, bringing my bottoms with him. His breath hitching when he noticed the surprise I had in store for him.

"Commando, huh? Were you playing with yourself in bed this morning?" he asked, grazing one finger over my slick folds.

I paused, before answering. "No," I said, weakly.

"Don't lie to me. Do you think about me when you're finger-fucking yourself, Cass? Because I think about you as I make myself come every night," Blake growled

Blake wasn't even touching me, and I thought I was coming unhinged. "Do you want to touch yourself now?" he asked.

"Mmmhmm," I groaned.

"Good because I want to see you touch yourself," he groaned.

At his request, I reached for my pussy. "Just not yet!" he rumbled.

"But, I thought," I sulked.

"Yes, but we're doing things on my terms," he said. "Doctor's orders, remember?"

"Now sit up on your elbows," he ordered, as I lifted my back off the mattress. "You're such a good patient, Cass," he added with a wink.

"Only because I have an amazing doctor. He takes such good care of me," I teased.

"Oh, Carpenter, you haven't seen anything yet. Now gently tease your right nipple."

Following his instructions, my breathing only intensified.

"How will this help my ankle, Doctor?" I asked through ragged breaths.

"Do you feel any pain right now?" he asked.

"Not in my ankle. But I need to touch myself, Blake! Please let me touch myself," I begged.

"OK, lay back down, and gently insert one finger. Use your other hand and play with your left breast. We have to give the girls both equal attention now," he said. "That's good just like that," he added, as I slid one finger back and forth, entering it deeper with each thrust.

"Add a second finger, and stroke your clit with your thumb," he said.

Concentrating on bringing myself to orgasm, I didn't notice when Blake walked over to my dresser and removed a vibrator from the top drawer. Stroking my clit, I was surprised when Blake ran the vibrator from the slit of my ass up to my glistening pussy where the vibration alone nearly rocketed me over the edge.

"How did you know that was in there?" I panted.

"Lucky guess, I suppose," he answered. "Now tell me, Carpenter, is this the guilty toy that caused your little mishap?"

"Yes," I answered.

"Do you like this toy?" he teased.

"Yes," I responded again, only able to form one-word answers. Spreading my legs farther apart, Blake took that as a sign and slammed the vibrator into my aching core causing my walls to immediately spasm around it.

"You're right," he said, as he continued to work my eager pussy with the vibe. "We're keeping these."

"I told you they were amazing," I screamed, curling my toes in anticipation of a second orgasm.

Chapter Seventeen

BLAKE

*A*FTER REUNITING WITH Cass for some quick role-playing in the bedroom, I came out into the living room to watch SportsCenter while she jumped in the shower. I'd tried to get her to agree to let me join her, but she refused saying that someone should be ready in case Kaity needed something.

Turning on the TV, my phone rang in my pocket. Looking at the caller ID, I didn't recognize the number, but saw it was someone from New York.

"Hello, this is Blake Mitchell," I said, answering the call.

"Hi, Mr. Mitchell, this is Barb calling from the New York County district attorney's office. We wanted to inform you that a plea has been reached in the case involving Alyssa Mitchell, and sentencing has been scheduled for April tenth at noon. The assistant prosecutor hopes that you'll be available to speak on behalf of the prosecution to ensure the defendant gets the longest possible sentence."

Swallowing back the lump that had formed in my throat, I agreed to fly back to New York for the hearing. "Yes, I'll be there, Barb. Thank you for the call."

"You're most welcome, Mr. Mitchell. Do you have any other questions that I might be able to answer for you today?" Barb asked.

"No, but if you could please forward the information to my e-mail that would be helpful," I requested.

"Not a problem, Sir. I believe we should have that on file here. If you think of anything else, please don't hesitate to call."

"Thank you, Barb. Have a nice weekend," I said, ending the call.

Sitting forward, I raked my fingers through my hair thinking about how the nightmare that I'd suffered over a year earlier would finally come to an end. Justice would finally prevail for Alyssa's death, and the bastard who'd killed her would finally end up behind bars–hopefully for many, many years if I could have anything to do with it.

Standing, I began pacing back and forth across the carpeted floor thinking about how I would react when I finally came face-to-face with the fucker who took my children's mother away from them. I'd have to tell the court what she meant to me, and to my family. How the most amazing woman, who had so much life ahead of her, had everything ripped away because someone else had one drunken afternoon and decided to get behind the wheel of a car.

After the accident, I didn't ask many questions–I didn't want to know a lot about him. Now I often found myself wondering about him. Did he have a family? A wife? Children? I wasn't sure why I cared, but I hoped he hadn't ruined their lives, too.

"You know, if you keep doing that you're going to wear a hole in my carpet," Cass said, breaking through my thoughts.

"Oh, right," I said, stopping in my tracks. "Sorry."

"Something wrong? You're not acting like the same guy I just left in the bedroom," she questioned.

Taking a seat back on the couch, I motioned for Cass to sit next to me. "I just got a call from the New York County DA's office. A plea has been reached with the bastard who killed Lys. They want me to come for the sentencing next month," I explained, resting my head in my palms.

"Oh," she said, her expression looking as if she were searching for the right words to say.

"It's OK, I don't really know what else to say either. I definitely wasn't expecting that call today. The last I heard, they were expecting the case to go to trial this summer."

"Are you OK with a plea deal?" she asked.

"The prosecution seemed to think it was favorable. If it were up to me, the guy would get the electric chair, but that's not how the system works. I guess as long as he spends a decent amount of time behind bars, and can't ruin someone else's family then I'm OK with it."

"I understand," she said, rubbing her hand up and down my back. "Is there anything I can do?"

"Actually, yeah, come to the sentencing with me?" I asked, surprising myself with the request as much as Cass.

She looked at me for a moment before answering. "If that's what you really want then I'll go with you, Blake," she said, resting her head against my shoulder.

"Thank you," I whispered, turning to place a kiss on top of her head. "I know it won't be an easy day, but with you by my side, I think it'll be just a bit more bearable."

CASSIDY

AFTER CURLING UP into Blake's arms for several hours as we watched TV, I realized it was approaching time for dinner. Since I didn't know that Blake would be here in time for a meal, I hadn't made reservations or bought any food in preparation.

"Do you just want to order out?" I asked, reaching for a folder filled with takeout menus. "I was thinking Chinese food sounded really good right now," I added, nearly salivating over the thought of an egg roll.

"Yeah, that sounds great to me, actually. I don't think I'm up to dealing with large crowds tonight anyways, and if we went grocery shopping I'd have to walk behind your slow motorized cart," he said, pinching me in the arm.

"Ouch!" I said, smacking him in the chest. "Why do you have to be so mean. You're never going to let me live this down, are you?" I added, rolling my eyes.

"Nope, it will forever be known as Dildogate," he said, a wide grin crossing his face.

"Oh my god," I said, covering my face. "You're an even bigger asshole than I thought."

"Maybe, but you love me," he joked with a shrug of the shoulders. Stilling at his words, I didn't know how to respond. He may have just been joking, but neither one of us had used the L-word, yet. Surely, I wasn't ready to start now, or was I? No, it was still too soon and much too complicated. After all, we still had those measly five-hundred miles between us.

Before I had much more time to think about it, there was a knock on the door. "I'll get it," Blake said, patting me on the leg. "I need you at full-strength tonight," he added with a sexy wink.

"Only if you're lucky," I said, tossing a throw pillow in his direction.

"Don't try out for quarterback, Carpenter," he snickered, as the pillow sailed passed him and ricocheted off the door.

"Daddy! Daddy!" I heard Maddy greet Blake as he opened the door.

"Hey, Baby Girl! Did you have a good time with Aunt Brooke and Uncle Rich?"

"Yeah, and Bwendan! I lubs him Daddy! I want to mawwy him!" she squealed in delight. I laughed knowing that Blake was squirming at her admission.

"Is that so?" he said, raising his brow, as Rich chuckled behind him. "You're not even three yet, Princess. I don't think you need to be thinking about marriage anytime soon."

"That's my son–already the little, ladies' man," Rich joked, as Maddy and Ben ran towards me.

"I don't think I want my daughter marrying any son of yours, Hot," Blake joked, slapping Rich on the shoulder.

"Do you two want to come in for a while? We were just about to order some Chinese food." Blake asked.

"Nah, thanks though. I made dinner reservations for Valentine's Day. You know like a real gentleman does for his woman," Rich teased.

Having to help Blake out, I screamed from the couch, "You'll never be a gentleman, Davis. And, trust me, Blake definitely knows how to please his woman."

"Well Brooke hasn't had any complaints either," Rich yelled back.

"Ha! Keep telling yourself that, Dick!"

"You sure you really want that chick?" Rich asked Blake, as I threw another pillow at the door. This one hitting Rich square in the face.

"Yeah, she's definitely a keeper," Blake laughed. "And, maybe not such a bad QB after all. Now, go, I'm sure your wife is growing impatient waiting for your ass. Do you two need us to watch Brendan tonight?"

"Nah, thanks for the offer through. My mom has been waiting to get her paws all over him for an entire night. She's been talking about it for weeks, but I couldn't get Brooke to give him up for a night. He's certainly been a little cockblocker that's for sure!"

"Welcome to parenthood, Man!" Blake said.

"Thanks, we'll catch you two later," Rich said, turning to leave.

"Bye, Dick!" I yelled before Blake shut the door.

"You're terrible," Blake laughed, turning back toward me as Kaity ran out from her bedroom.

"Hey Maddy! Hi Ben!" Kaity said, giving them both hugs, nearly toppling them over.

"Hey, Baby, can you please help Maddy and Ben wash their hands before dinner?" I asked, smothering her face in kisses.

"Sure, Mommy, but you're being silly!" she said, squirming out of my embrace.

"Mommy, just loves you, that's all," I said.

"I love you, too, Mommy. Now, come on, Maddy. Let's go, Ben!" she ordered, taking her task seriously. In just a few short months, she'd definitely taken on the role of a big sister and quickly emerged as the little leader of the bunch. The girls ran ahead of Ben as he took several short steps trying to keep up. Blake had told me how far along Ben had come with his walking in just the month since I'd seen him. He was still waiting for Ben to say his first word amongst all his baby chatter.

"I think I need a nap after just watching those three. What's it like to have that much energy?" I laughed.

"Now you know why I have to hit the gym seven days a week? I wouldn't be able to keep up with those two otherwise."

"And, here I thought you were just doing it to keep up with me in the bedroom."

"Keep up with that sassy mouth and no one will be eating dinner," Blake warned, drawing me in for a kiss.

"OK, Mommy! We all washed our hands," Kaity yelled, as the troops all ran back into the room.

"Ewwww," she said, catching Blake and me in a kiss. "Mommy! Boys have cooties! At least all of the boys at my school do!"

"Baby, in about fifty years, you might actually like a boy and want to leave your mommy," I explained. "Now will you help me set the table?"

"Fifty years?" Blake teased.

"What? You just nearly had a heart attack when your daughter said she loved Brendan," I said, shrugging.

"She's not even three! You're implying that Kaity can't date until she's fifty-five," he laughed.

"You're right. Maybe I'm being ridiculous. I suppose I'd be OK if she dated at forty."

WE'D JUST FINISHED the last of the fried rice, empty containers strewn all about the table, when Ben placed his chubby hand on my arm, wanting out of his high chair.

"Hey there, Big Guy," I said, patting him on top of his head. "Do you want to sit on my lap?"

He nodded, as I plucked him out of the chair, sitting him on my lap. Bouncing him up and down for several seconds, his laughter filled the room. "Mamma, Mamma," he yelled, as I looked toward Blake, not sure he'd heard the words his son had spoken.

Blake quickly rose from his chair, clearly as shaken as I was by his son's first word.

"I really thought he was going to say 'Dadda'. That was Maddy's first word, you know. Alyssa was so mad. She wouldn't talk to me for hours," Blake laughed at the memory. "Maybe this is her way of getting back at me–ironic, isn't it?"

"Blake, maybe he said 'Maddy'? Or, maybe it was just baby talk," I said, trying to ease the situation.

"Mamma, Mamma," Ben screeched, once again.

Blake turned to his son who was still sitting on my lap. "No, Cass, he thinks you're his momma," he said, taking him in his arms. "He's probably just copying Kaity. It's no big deal," he added, shrugging his shoulders.

"Come on, Little Man, let's put you down for the night," he said, carrying Ben to the spare bedroom where he'd set up a pack 'n play.

I watched as Blake carried Ben down the hallway. "Dadda, can you say Dadda?"

Blake may have told me that it wasn't a big deal, but his actions said otherwise. He was definitely unnerved by the situation. Truthfully, so was I. As much as I didn't want to let it bother me, I'd always have Alyssa's ghost hanging over me.

Chapter Eighteen

WITH MY ANKLE healing and the height of the wedding season right around the corner, I hadn't had been able to take a trip to D.C. for St. Paddy's Day for the annual parade and festivities like I'd originally planned. Instead Blake and I had to go nearly two months without seeing each other. Even though we talked at least once each day on the phone, the distance was really starting to take its toll on our relationship–especially with the impending court date lingering on our minds.

I'd come into the office to meet with a new client before Blake was expected to get into town later in the day. He'd promised to take the kids and me to the local street fair before flying with me to New York for the sentencing date. He knew I wasn't a fan of flying the friendly skies, especially alone, and he remembered my last incident with the Prosecco.

Hearing the doors to my office jingling, I quickly ended a conference call with a few of my distributors.

"Be right there," I yelled, quickly reapplying my lip gloss.

Hurrying out into the front portion of my office, I was surprised to see a familiar face along with a beautiful, big-breasted blonde. A perfect Trophy Wife for the Major League superstar.

"Well, if it isn't Jason James," I said, as the two stood by the door.

"Cassidy Carpenter," he said, outstretching his hand. "I tried to convince my fiancée to go to another wedding planner, but she insisted that you were the very best."

"Well, Jason, it looks like you somehow managed to snag a smart woman," I said, sarcastically. I wanted to tell him not to fuck this one up, but I bit my lip, trying to remain professional.

Jason had been Brooke's high school sweetheart until he was caught cheating on her and broke her heart while we were in college. As much as I harassed Rich for not being good enough for my best friend, he was a saint in comparison to Jason–at least in my eyes.

Brooke, however, had forgiven him, and even agreed to briefly date the guy when she and Rich had separated for a brief period. Truthfully, I guess Brooke's just a better person than I am because I was cheering Rich on when he came back and threatened to punch Jason in the nuts. I was only disappointed that Dick hadn't followed through with it.

"So, Jason, you actually convinced this beautiful woman to marry you, huh?" I said with a forced smile.

"He did," she giggled, clearly nervous with our uncomfortable exchange. "Maybe you were right, Babe. Maybe we should go see someone else," she said.

Although the thought of planning Jason's wedding made me want to blow chucks all over his expensive loafers, this was an opportunity I couldn't pass up. I mean he had become a face of baseball especially after his trade to the Cubs last year. His career was suddenly taking off from an average utility player to an everyday outfielder known for his strong bat.

"Don't be silly," I said, forcing a fake smile. "I'd actually be honored to plan your wedding. At least we know it'll cost a mint and be beautiful."

"Well, fantastic," she said. "And, I don't think we've been properly introduced, I'm Tara."

"It's a pleasure to meet you, Tara," I said, shaking her hand. Just as I was going to escort the two back to my office, the door opened, and in walked my handsome man.

"Hey!" I said, a real smile forming across my face. "I didn't expect to see you until dinner. As you can see, I'm with a client, but I shouldn't be much longer."

"Hey, yourself," he said, kissing me on the cheek. "Take your time. Rich and Brooke are already at the fair with the kids. I can go on ahead, and you can just meet up with us when you're done. If that's cool with you?"

Before I had a chance to respond, a look of recognition swept across Blake's face. "I'm sorry, but are you Jason James?" he asked. "Babe, do you know who this is?"

"Yep, it's Jason James, and yes, I know who he is," I said, rolling my eyes.

"Dude, I'm a huge fan. I followed you when you were with the Marlins, but I've heard you really give the Cubs a good chance at a title," Blake said, shaking Jason's hand.

"Here's an interesting little fact. Did you know Jason here cheated on Brooke?" I asked, momentarily forgetting my professionalism.

"Brooke, Brooke?" Blake asked. "Brooke dated Jason James?"

"It was a long time ago," Jason interjected. "And, for what it's worth, I really do regret hurting Brooke. I was young and dumb. I'd like to think I've learned from my mistakes," Jason said.

"Cut the guy some slack, Cass. We've all made mistakes," he said, suddenly Jason's biggest supporter.

"Hey, thanks, Man!" Jason said, fist-bumping Blake. "Hey,

why don't you two get to the fair. We can just reschedule our appointment, right Tara?"

"Oh, yeah, sure thing," Tara replied, as she flipped through some bridal magazines I'd set out.

"Are you driving, or should I?" I asked after rescheduling my appointment with Jason and Tara.

"I was thinking we could just skip the carnival, and we could get naked in your office," Blake suggested, wagging his brows.

"You actually think you're getting lucky after you just stuck up for Jason like that? I asked. "You must've gotten hit in the head because I know you aren't that dumb."

"Seriously? But, Cass, I haven't seen you in two months. My blue balls have blue balls," he deadpanned. "I'll just shoot Rich a text and tell him your appointment ran longer than expected and we'll just meet them back at the house for dinner."

"Yes, seriously! You should've thought about your nuts before you went fist-bumping that loser. Besides, I really wanted some carnival fries, and a funnel cake," I pouted.

"I promise, once I'm fucking you over the desk, you'll forget all about Jason James, French fries and funnel cakes," he said, seductively.

"Wh—what were we talking about?" I asked, already weak in the knees.

"That's my girl," he said, scooping me into his arms and carrying me into the office where he shut and locked the door behind us.

AFTER BLAKE HAD bent me over the desk, and properly fucked me not once, but twice, and then for a third time against the wall, we'd made it back to my apartment just ahead of Rich, Brooke, and the kids. I was sure I was going to get the inquisition from

Brooke as to why we ditched them at the fair. Feeling guilty for leaving my now pregnant best friend with four kids, I vowed to not dismiss her questions.

Shortly after Brendan's adoption became official, Brooke learned that she was pregnant with twins. Because of her previous complications, the two opted to not tell anyone until Brooke was further along in her pregnancy, but now that she'd surpassed the first trimester they were able to more easily relax and start sharing their miraculous news.

"Looks like you and Blake are getting along well. He can't keep his eyes off you," Brooke swooned as we sat at the kitchen island drinking mocktails. The boys had agreed to take the kids into the living room so we could have our girl time. I think they both thought it would improve their chances at scoring later.

"Yeah, things have been going as well as they can be considering we still live over five-hundred miles apart," I sighed, answering her question.

"Cassidy Carpenter, do I sense that you'd actually like more?"

"I didn't say that, but it'd be nice to have the option."

"Have you two talked about him moving here?" she questioned.

"No, he just moved to D.C. I highly doubt moving to Michigan is really in his plans right now. Besides, I don't think your husband would be very pleased with me if I went and stole his star reporter out from under him."

"Actually, you didn't hear this from me, but Rich is probably taking a position in Detroit. He's tired of spending so much time away from us especially with the pregnancy. I suspect he'll be here in Michigan full-time within the next month," Brooke said.

"Really? Does Blake know?" I asked.

"Yeah, he told him yesterday. Rich feels bad about it because he got him to move to D.C. Rich thinks he'll get promoted to editor though once he's gone, but maybe he'll actually want to move with him," Brooke suggested.

I sighed knowing I couldn't expect him to pass up the opportunity to become the next editor of the *Post*. "I can't ask him to give that up for me, Brooke," I said, sadness in my voice. "

"Cass, you aren't asking him to give up something that he might not want anyways. Did you even stop to consider that possibility?"

"It doesn't matter. Right now, the only thing that matters is getting through this sentencing. Maybe once that isn't hanging over our heads then we can talk about what's next for us."

"You love him don't you?" Brooke questioned.

"I haven't told him that, no!" I whisper-yelled.

"I didn't ask you if you'd told him. I asked you if you did, but I think that's answer enough for me," she said, her mouth twisting into a smirk.

Noticing Blake come up behind us, I nudged Brooke in the arm. "Shhhh," I said, putting my finger to my lips.

"What are you two beautiful ladies discussing?" Blake asked while taking the empty stool beside me.

Looking at Brooke, I silently prayed that she would keep my secret. "Nothing. Just a little girl talk is all," Brooke explained.

"Mmmhmm, I think that is code for we're not telling you," Blake said with a wink.

"You're a smart man, Blake. I think you could give my husband a few pointers," Brooke joked. "Right, Babe," she added, yelling into the living room.

"Sure, whatever you say, Sweets," Rich yelled back, not having any idea what he was agreeing to.

"You want to know the best part about being pregnant?" Brooke asked. "He doesn't argue with me about anything anymore."

"Wait a second, are you telling me that Hot has grown a pussy?" Blake laughed.

"Very funny, Asshole," Rich yelled, taking a seat at the island next to Brooke. "My dick is still very much intact, and in working order. In fact, I even have solid evidence," he added, rubbing Brooke's small bump.

Just as we were sitting down to eat, I remembered I hadn't told Brooke about my visitor earlier in the day.

"Hey Brookie, you'll never guess who'll be needing my wedding planning expertise," I said.

"Yeah? Who?" she asked, her curiosity piqued.

"Jason James," I said, raising my brow.

"No shit," she said, seemingly unimpressed. "Well, good for him, I guess."

"I should make sure his tux comes in two sizes too small in the inseam. Make him get married with his pants cupping his junk," I laughed.

"Cass, for once, I think I like the way you think," Rich said, suddenly interested in the conversation.

Chapter Nineteen

BLAKE

WALKING INTO THE kitchen, I noticed Cass swaying her hips as she cleaned up after our dinner party. There wasn't actually any music playing so she must've had something stuck in her head. She stopped for a moment to unhook the top few buttons of her shirt and splash some water on her face. I wasn't sure how she did it, but she managed to turn the simplest of tasks into my very own personal porno.

Tucking my arms across my chest, I propped myself against the door frame to take in the show. I was creepin' and I didn't even care. She looked hot as fuck in her fitted shirt and short, little shorts which showed off the swell of her ass. My cock was already throbbing and she hadn't even turned in my direction. A moan escaped me when her hip-swaying turned into more of a bootie pop, causing her to finally turn to face me.

"Finally come in to help me clean?" she asked, tossing a wet rag in my direction.

"No, I was thinking it was time for some dessert," I said, stalking toward her with the dishcloth still in my hands.

"Stop it! You're going to get me all wet," she laughed, as I pinned her body against the kitchen island.

"That's the idea," I growled.

She rolled her eyes before responding, "You're nothing but trouble." Then she smirked, her face beginning to blush. "And, you turned down dessert when the rest of us ate it. Something about it spoiling your diet?" she smiled, lifting my shirt to rub her fingers across my abs.

My breath hitched at her touch. "I'm not talking about the chocolate cake, Carpenter, but something tells me you already knew that," I hissed, grabbing a handful of ass as I lifted her to the countertop.

"We can't do this, Blake. Not with the kids in the other room," she reminded me. I smiled knowing the little cockblockers wouldn't be a problem tonight.

This would be fun. I secretly loved getting a rise out of my girl. "I can be quiet. The question is, can you?" I whispered, as I bit down softly on her ear.

Moaning, she dropped her head back allowing me to place a trail of kisses down her neck. I then guided my hands to her abdomen where I began unbuttoning her shirt.

"Blake, stop!" she squealed through heated breaths. "The kids!"

It was time to let Cass in on my little secret if I was going to relieve this bulge in my pants tonight. "I sent the kids home with Rich and Brooke."

"What? Kaity too?" she asked.

"Kaity too." I said, popping the last button of her shirt to expose her lacy white bra. "I hope you're not mad. I just wanted us to be alone tonight." She didn't hesitate as she pulled up the hem of my shirt and once again began tracing my abs with her finger. I couldn't stand any more of her slow torture. Yanking my shirt over my head, I tossed it to the floor.

"I'm definitely not mad about that," she said, desire burning in her eyes. "I just wish you'd told me sooner. Now stop teasing me, and get to work," she ordered, lying back on the island.

"I haven't even begun to tease you yet, Baby," I whispered, as I slid my hand under her bra, lightly brushing my finger over her already pert nipple. "I've been watching you all day and dreaming about taking you nice and slow all night long."

Wrapping her legs around my torso, my cock pulsated from her closeness. She knew what she was doing to me, but I stuck to my guns. Tonight was about taking it slow–showing her how much I cared about her.

"Take me to the bedroom, Blake, please," she begged through shallow breaths.

"No, I think we'll stay right here. After all, we eat our dessert in the kitchen," I teased, reaching for the bottle of chocolate syrup that she'd yet to put away.

Her eyes widened, "You're not actually going to get chocolate on me are you?"

I nodded, tracing my tongue over my lips.

"You're going to get me filthy!" she squealed.

"That's the plan, Baby," I said, squirting chocolate on her stomach. She arched her back as I began to lick the chocolate in a line from her navel toward her breasts, stopping when I reached her bra.

"Jesus! Why are you stopping? I think you're trying to kill me," she panted.

Cass was always sexy in my eyes, but angry Cass was even sexier. Her face down to her neck had flushed and a shimmer of perspiration outlined her chest. Her lips were turned into the cutest, little pout and her eyes were smoldering. Her normally transparent blue orbs replaced with opaque black marbles. I had a feeling she was about to win this battle. I wouldn't be able to hold out much longer, and we weren't even naked yet.

Sit up," I ordered. Without hesitation, she obeyed my command. Pulling off her already undone shirt, I made quick work of removing her bra. I moaned as her tits sprang free, her swollen nipples already standing at full attention.

"Lie back down and lift your hips," I instructed. Once again, she responded without hesitation allowing me to work open the button on her shorts. Sliding them down, I guffawed when I noticed Cass had left me with a little surprise. Her bottom bare beneath her shorts–her pussy on full display, awaiting my touch.

"Like what you see, Mr. Mitchell?" she giggled, spreading her legs a little wider. "I may have let you win this battle, but the war will always be mine," she winked, kicking off her shorts with one flick of the legs.

For a moment, I was ready to raise the white flag in surrender and drop my pants, filling her completely. Letting out a deep breath, I cleared my head and remembered my mantra for the night–nice and slow. After all, it wasn't very often that we were without all three kids for an entire night. The pleasure would definitely be worth the pain I was currently feeling down below.

"Keep those legs spread. I'll be right back," I said, walking away from the island.

"Where–where are you going?" She asked through ragged breaths.

"I think I'm in the mood for something more than just chocolate for dessert," I teased, walking over to the fridge to grab the can of whipped cream. "I'm thinking about my very own sundae."

Stalking back toward her, I couldn't take it any longer. I had to taste her. Giving the can a quick shake, I tipped it over to outline the lips of her pussy. Momentarily pausing to enjoy the view, I quickly dropped my head to her core tracing her outer lips with my tongue.

"God. Please Blake! Harder! You win! I need to come–now!"

she yelled out.

At her request, I delved my tongue into her center, sucking and swirling her clit. After just a few moments, her hips began to buck and she screamed in pleasure. I continued my assault on her pussy until she came down from her orgasmic high.

Standing above her, I took pleasure in the faint smile on her lips. She slowly sat up, my eyes fixed on her heavy chest. "Can I have a taste?" she asked, pulling my lips toward hers.

This time it was her turn to assault me. Her lips sucking the mixture of her wetness and whipped cream off mine. Kissing my lips, her hands worked to unfasten my belt.

"I think it's time to take this to the bedroom," I breathed through heated kisses. "I think I'm done with taking this slow. It's time to show you how hard I can be."

"I think that sounds perfect," Cass answered, wrapping herself around my torso. "Take me to the bedroom!"

"Your wish is my command," I laughed, squeezing the firm globes of her ass.

CASSIDY

"SHOWER," I PANTED as Blake feverishly attacked my lips.

"Uh-uh, sex then shower," he moaned. "I need to bury myself in you–now!"

"Shower sex?" I asked, raising a brow. "Think about it. It's the best of both worlds."

By the expression on his face, I knew I had him. There was no denying I was right about that.

"Although I like the way you think, Baby, there's one problem," he replied.

"What's that?"

"I might bust a nut just thinking about water cascading down these perfect tits," he moaned as he began feasting on my hardened nipples.

"Shower, now, please" I begged, arching my back as he carried me into the bathroom.

Blake sat me down on the vanity as he made quick work of removing his jeans, the tip of his cock springing free from the band of his briefs.

"Come here," I requested, motioning towards him with my finger. "I can't wait any longer either."

He came toward me like a lion stalking its prey, like he was starving and I was his last supper.

Reaching for the tip of his cock, I swirled my finger around the head before lowering his briefs enough to free his length. Guiding his cock with my hands, I placed it at my center, begging him with my eyes to enter.

Gone was the slow and gentle Blake of earlier. Without wasting a second, he placed his hands under my ass, lifting me slightly before plowing into me and leaving me gasping for air. Only taking a moment for my walls to mold around him, he filled me completely as he continued pumping into me further. Looking into the floor-length mirror positioned behind Blake, I watched as he buried himself balls-deep into my pussy. It was the most erotic sight I'd ever seen.

"Harder, harder," I screamed.

He kept a rigorous pace, and after only a few minutes I could tell that he was getting close to his release. Using the counter to create friction, I rocked back and forth in order to speed up my own orgasm as he continued to thrust his hard cock into my wet, slippery core.

Bending down, he began nipping on my breasts. The double pleasure was too much and he soon sent me over the edge, my walls tightening and spasming around his girth. Slamming into me once more, Blake growled as he let go of his own release.

Flinging my head back, I sat motionless for several seconds trying to catch my breath.

"Looks like we didn't make it to the shower after all," Blake joked, breaking the silence.

"I thought we could save it for round two. Why don't you turn on the water," I sassed, playfully.

"Woman, if I didn't know any better I'd think you were trying to kill me," he said, turning on the faucet.

After Blake had properly pleasured me in the shower, and twice more in bed, I was spent. We spooned against each other for several minutes before Blake got up to use the bathroom. Lying in bed alone, my mind began swirling about what was actually happening between us.

We'd been casually seeing each other for quite some time now, but we hadn't officially put a label on anything. I know he was faithful to me, just as I was faithful to him, but Blake insisted that he didn't want to rush me into anything, but tonight definitely felt more intimate–more like we were making love.

Taking a deep breath, I sunk my head further into the pillow. Does Blake love me? Do I love Blake? My mind continued to race as I heard Blake come back into the room.

"You still awake?" he asked, the mattress sinking from his weight.

"Mmmhmm," I mumbled, rolling to my side.

"I think we should talk," he whispered.

Those were five words a girl never wanted to hear–especially with the significance of the next few days lingering over our heads. Nothing good ever came out of a conversation that began with those five words. How did I get things so wrong? Here I thought tonight meant something more while Blake was simply telling me goodbye. I got close to another man just for him to break my heart too.

"Cass, did you hear me?" he asked again. Instead of responding, I closed my eyes and let sleep take me away. I'd leave the goodbyes for another day.

"I think I'm falling in love with you," Blake whispered as I slept.

Chapter Twenty

CASSIDY

AFTER MORE THAN a year in the court system, the asshole who'd taken Alyssa's life would finally be sentenced today. It may have been selfish of me, but I was relieved when Blake told me the news that a plea bargain had been accepted. I feared what a trial may have done to our relationship–those demons and memories haunting us.

Blake didn't talk much about the accident, and I didn't want to pry. He'd been much better in the last few months opening up about his past with Alyssa, and I didn't want to halt the progress we'd made. The very few details I knew about her death, I'd either gotten from Brooke, or from the Internet. I knew the man who'd killed Alyssa, Quint Michaelson, had a history of DUIs and didn't even have a valid license at the time of the accident.

At first, I was hurt that Blake hadn't confided in me. I was fearful that he'd run, just like every man before him. But, in the months we'd been together, he'd proven time and time again that he wasn't like those other men. With each passing day, I was learning to trust Blake more and more. And, even though, neither of us had spoken the words, I knew I was in love with him.

Assuming it would be something he'd rather do alone, I was

surprised when he'd asked me to travel back to New York with him for the sentencing.

After falling asleep in Blake's arms, the night before last, we woke as if Blake had never mentioned needing to talk. I certainly didn't want to press the issue, especially with the added stress of this day weighing him down. Truthfully, I was relieved when he seemed to have forgotten all about it.

Arriving at the courthouse more than forty-five minutes early, we checked through security and made our way into the empty courtroom. I took a seat on a long, wooden bench as Blake paced the length of the aisle, fidgeting with the knot of his tie.

Although we weren't in the ideal location, I still took note of how delicious he looked wearing a light blue, button-down shirt which hugged his muscular arms and thick neck, and khaki slacks which perfectly outlined his trim waist. I watched him for a moment longer, thinking about what those same clothes would look like heaped on the bedroom floor, when he finally stopped, glancing in my direction.

"What's on your mind?" he questioned, catching me in my gaze.

"Nothing, it's not important," I said, giving a half-smile. "Why don't you sit down? You're making me nervous with your pacing," I added, patting the spot next to me.

"I just don't think I can sit right now. Honestly, I feel like I'm going to be sick," he admitted, exhaling sharply.

"I'm sorry," I said in a dull voice. "Is there anything I can do to make it better?"

"You're already making it better just because you're here. I don't know how I could be doing this right now without you," he said, sincerity in his tone.

"I'll stay by your side for as long as you need me to be," I said, standing to place a soft kiss on his cheek.

"Thank you," he mouthed, as an assistant district attorney entered the courtroom.

"Mr. Mitchell?" she asked. "Would you follow me to the conference room so we can prepare you for the judge's questions?"

"Certainly, I'll be right behind you," he said, as he lightly squeezed my face, pecking me on the forehead. "Do you want to stay here? I'll just be a few minutes."

"Sure, that's fine. I'm not going anywhere. I'll just keep our places," I said with a weak laugh.

Staring at the clock, I watched a few minutes tick by. Since it was policy that cellphones and other devices weren't allowed in the courtroom, time seamed to pass by at a much slower pace. Picking a piece of lint from my black pencil skirt, I looked up as I heard the courtroom door open.

First entering the courtroom was the one who I believed was the defendant's attorney. He was a good-looking man, probably a few years older than I with salt and pepper hair. He looked distinguished, a little like George Clooney, the exact definition of a silver fox. Following closely behind him, escorted by a police officer, was the defendant himself.

Seeing this man for the first time, dressed all in orange, I blinked rapidly hoping my mind was just playing tricks on me–the stress of the day finally taking its toll. Staring at him with my mouth agape, he finally looked in my direction–recognition sweeping across his face.

"No, no, no. This can't be happening. That man is not Quint Michaelson," I said to myself, as the room began spinning around me.

Needing air, I dashed toward the exit just as Blake and the DA were entering the courtroom.

"Whoa, Cass, are you OK?" Blake asked, catching me in his arms. "You look like you've seen a ghost."

If he only knew the truth behind his words, although maybe not a ghost, but more like a monster. "I–I need some air, maybe a glass of water. I'll–I'll be right back," I stuttered, my entire body beginning to quake.

"I'll go with you. You can tell me what's going on with you," he said, worry written on his face.

"Mr. Mitchell, I'm sorry, but you can't leave right now. The judge is about to enter and you'll be called to the witness stand first," the DA said, listening in on our conversation.

He looked at me for a moment before turning back to the DA. "I'm sorry, but I need to be with her," he said, opening the door for me.

"No, Blake, you need to stay here. You need to do this for Alyssa. You need to do this for me," I nearly begged.

Confusion flashed across his face, "OK, you know I'll do anything for you, but I don't understand what this has to do with you?" he said.

"Just stay. Please just stay here. I'll be fine," I pleaded, trying to conceal my anguish.

Truthfully, I wasn't fine. The baggage that I'd carried around for years had just shown up at my doorstep. The demons I'd tried to bury when I'd met Blake had just resurfaced. I was sure he would never forgive me for this. I had to leave before I could give him the chance to leave me.

Convincing Blake to stay in the courtroom, just as the judge was about to enter the chamber, I ran into the restroom and splashed cold water on my face. Staring at my reflection, I didn't even recognize myself in the mirror. Gone was the confident woman who'd overcome her fears, and who at last had given love a chance. She'd been replaced with her former shell, the woman who just lived day by day, not letting anyone get too close.

Knowing court would be in session for at least an hour, I

slipped out of the courthouse, hailing the first taxi that came into view. Sliding into the back seat, I asked the driver to take me back to the hotel so I could grab my things, and get the hell out of this city. I couldn't be around Quint Michaelson, the name Steve was going by these days. And as much as I wanted the comfort of Blake's arms wrapped around me, I knew he wouldn't want anything to do with me once he learned the ugly truth about his wife's killer.

Pulling up to the hotel entrance, I asked the driver to wait for me while I went in to grab my suitcases. Knowing I didn't have much time before Blake came looking for me, I scurried around the room trying to remain calm. Throwing my bags into the trunk, and sliding back into the taxi, I finally reached for my phone, noticing I already had two missed calls from Blake. Not bothering to open my voicemails, I quickly dialed Brooke.

"Cass?" she answered, alarm in her voice.

"Yeah, it's me," I responded.

"What the hell is going on with you? Blake just called me in a panic telling me that you just up and left the courthouse without so much as a goodbye. He has no idea what's wrong!" she yelled into the phone. "Have you lost your damn mind?"

Taking a deep breath, "I guess you could say that—at least I thought I was losing it when I saw Quint Michaelson for the first time," I explained.

"I don't understand. The guy who killed Lys? What does he have to do with any of this?" she asked.

"Brooke, Quint Michaelson is Steve. It must be his alias, or something, because Quint Michaelson is really Steve Jackson. Or maybe Steven Jackson is really Quint Michaelson. Regardless, my baby's father killed Maddy and Ben's mother," I told her, tears by now streaming down my cheeks.

She gasped, "What? Are you sure?"

"Yes, I'm positive. You should've seen the look on his face when he saw me in the courtroom, Brookie. I just keep replaying it over and over in my head. It was a nightmare!"

"Cass, you need to calm down," she said, trying to soothe me. "Where are you now? Wherever you are, just wait for Blake."

"No, no, no! You can't let Blake know where I am. He'll hate me, Brooke. He'll resent Kaity for being a part of HIM. I love Blake and he's going to reject me. I should've told him sooner, but I didn't. I was afraid, and now it's over and he'll never know how much he really meant to me–to us."

"He won't hate you. He only loves you, Cass," Brooke said, trying her best to reassure me.

"He may have loved me before, but he certainly won't after he learns the truth," I protested, my voice revealing defeat. "Please, just promise me you won't tell him that I'm at the airport. I need to be hundreds of miles away before I can even bear to talk to him. Promise me."

"Fine, I promise. Text me with your flight information and we'll come get you when you land," she said.

"It's fine. It might be late. I can just take an Uber."

"You aren't shutting me out, too, Cass. Text me!" she said, sternly.

"Fine. I love you, Brookie," I said.

"I love you, too," she replied, ending the call.

AFTER BOARDING THE plane, I finally decided to listen to the four voice messages from Blake after he realized I'd left the courthouse–with each message, his voice becoming more and more frantic. Knowing that I couldn't talk to him, but I didn't want to worry him either, I typed out a quick text before powering off the phone.

Cass: Blake, I'm sorry that I left you alone in that courtroom when you probably needed me the most. I didn't mean to hurt you. In case Brooke hasn't already told you, which I'm assuming she did, Quint Michaelson is actually an alias for Steve Jackson. Yes, the same Steve Jackson who left me pregnant with Kaitlyn. The same Steve Jackson who left me unable to trust any other men—until you. You were able to break down my walls, and help me to believe. I know this is all coming as a shock to you, and I understand that you'll never want to see me again. Seeing me would just be a painful reminder for everything that you've lost—everything your children have lost. Just know, I love you—I know I waited too long to tell you, but I do love you—I probably always will. Please don't come after me, I'll be OK. This will be best for all of us. Kiss those babies for me. Goodbye, Blake.

Even though I'd said goodbye before, this one seemed like the most difficult.

Chapter Twenty-One

BLAKE

*T*WELVE YEARS–MY SON would be in middle school, and my daughter might possibly be a cheerleader, going out on first dates, and attending high school dances while Quint Michaelson would be finishing the remainder of his sentence for killing my wife and their mother. As soon as the judge handed down his sentencing, I was relieved. Although I would never forget Quint Michaelson, or the pain he inflicted on my family, I could finally move forward with my life–my future with Cass. I would never have to hear his name again.

Leaving the courtroom, I expected to see Cass sitting on one of the benches, but she was nowhere to be found inside the building. She wasn't waiting for me outside either. Ever since I'd realized Cass was gone, I'd been searching the city for her. I thought maybe she'd been to the places that we'd visited, during her recent trip. I stopped at the various stores and boutiques along Fifth Avenue, Serendipity, and even McPherson's. But, she'd seemingly vanished into thin air.

Taking the stand to tell the court about my wife, my first love, I couldn't avoid the nagging feeling that something had gone terribly wrong with Cass. When I'd left her in the court chamber, she seemed like herself, so I couldn't quite piece together what may have happened in the short time I'd been gone. Was it Kaity? Her parents? Brooke?

Dozens of possible scenarios swirled through my mind. Had our relationship, hearing me talk about Alyssa, become too much for her? Had she gotten sick? The possibilities were endless, but none were as wild as learning the shocking truth several hours later, and by a text message no less.

While answering each question from the prosecution, I'd kept my eyes focused on the door, waiting for Cass to come back, but she never did. The moment I'd been able to power on my phone, I was surprised that she hadn't so much as sent a text to tell me she was all right. Calling Brooke, I was even more alarmed when she hadn't heard from Cass either. The last time I couldn't get ahold of someone I loved, my life as I knew it crumbled before me, and I wasn't sure if I was strong enough to survive it a second time.

Reclining in my chair, I'd just finished a conference call regarding a business piece I was working on when two of my officer buddies from my rookie days of covering the city's police beat showed up at my office door.

"Hey fellas, I think you're in the wrong place. The donut shop is next door," I joked.

The two didn't crack a smile, as they spoke the words that no man is ever prepared to hear.

"Blake, it's about your wife, Alyssa. She's been involved in a serious accident and has been taken to Mount Sinai," they said.

"What? I don't understand, I just talked to her a few hours ago. She was about to go Christmas shopping," I said, as I reached for my phone, dialing Alyssa's number. "This is a terrible joke," I added, her phone going straight to voicemail.

"Blake, we wouldn't joke about this. We wanted to be the ones to come here and tell you so you wouldn't hear it from a couple of strangers. You really need to get to the hospital right away. We were told she's

critical."

"Oh god! Do you know if she was alone?" I asked, remembering Alyssa was planning on dropping our daughter off at my parents' place. "And our baby? She's pregnant!"

"Yes, as far as we know, she was alone in the car. She was broadsided, and evidence gathered at the scene suggests that alcohol may have been a factor. We don't have any information on the baby, Blake. We just recommend you get to the hospital. I'm sure the doctors can answer all your questions. Do you have someone you can call for a ride, or would you like us to take you. You probably shouldn't be driving."

"I'll be fine," I said, resting my head in my palms.

Nodding in understanding, the officers left, allowing me to gather my thoughts. Threading my fingers through my hair, I had to process what was happening. Alyssa had to be OK, she just had to be for her own sake, for my family's sake, and for our unborn child's sake.

Not knowing where else to turn, I quickly dialed Rich's number even though he'd been going through a bunch of shit in his personal life. I needed my friend. After several rings, he finally answered the call.

"Rich! I need you," I said, screaming into the phone.

"I'm here. I'm here. What the fuck's wrong? You're scaring me."

"It's Alyssa. She's been in an accident. Fucking drunk driver. She was rushed to Mount Sinai. I don't have much more information. I could really use a friend, Man," I said, my heart thumping out of my chest.

"I'll be on the first flight out. Please give your beautiful wife a kiss for me. She's a fighter, Blake. You both need to fight—fight for her," he said, before ending the call.

Sitting on a bench outside the courthouse, I thought about Rich's words. Alyssa had been a fighter. She fought long and hard enough to keep our son alive; Now it was my turn to fight for Cass.

Preparing to call every hospital and police department within a fifty-mile radius to search for her, my phone dinged with an incoming text. Looking down, I sighed in relief when I saw her name flash across my screen.

Opening the text, I was unprepared for what I was about to read. Even among the wildest scenarios that I could've imagined for Cass's disappearance, I never would've guessed what she told me. How could Quint Michaelson be Steve Jackson–the Steve Jackson? Believing that Cass had to be mistaken, I quickly dialed the prosecutor, hoping to gain some clarity, and put Cass's mind to ease. The stress of the court proceedings must've affected her as much as it did me. That was the only logical explanation–it had to be.

Ending the call, I couldn't believe the words the attorney had told me. Quint Michaelson did at one point use the alias Steve Jackson for business purposes while living in the state of Michigan. He'd ended up in legal trouble for several driving offenses, one of which included drinking and driving, and ended up returning to his given name and moving to New York where his sister now lived.

Knowing the truth, I couldn't let Cass leave New York. We needed to talk about the situation. Although it was far from ideal, it didn't matter to me. In fact, knowing the truth, I just wished the fucker would serve more than twelve years behind bars–for not just his crime against my family, but for the pain he'd caused Cass and Kaity as well.

Dialing her number, I prayed she didn't get on that plane, but I knew she had when the call went straight to voicemail. My suspicions were confirmed when I got back to the hotel and found she'd taken all of her things.

Collapsing on the edge of the bed in defeat, a sinking feeling swept over me as I realized Cass actually believed I would hold her responsible for Alyssa's death. In my eyes, Cass and Kaity were just as much victims of Quint Michaelson as Alyssa, but

Cass didn't seem to believe enough in us to stick around and let me explain that to her. If she truly loved me as she said she did, she would've fought for me–she would've fought for us. Instead she dismissed me with nothing but a text message as a goodbye.

After dialing Cass's phone for several hours and it going straight to voicemail, I was shocked when it actually connected.

"Hi," she answered, barely above a whisper.

"You left," I said. After rehearsing this conversation in my head for the past three hours, I'd already forgotten everything I'd wanted to tell her.

"I'm sorry," she responded, her voice shaking.

"You didn't even give me the opportunity to fight for you. You just left. You cared so little about me, and what we've built that you just left. You didn't fight," I said calmly, rubbing a hand over my face. "Why didn't you put up fight?"

"There's nothing to fight about, Blake! My daughter's father killed your wife. How could you ever get past that? How could you ever look at her the same way? Look at me the same way?" she cried.

"Cass, I don't think you understand. I. Don't. Care! You actually think I would look at your little girl any differently than I already do? Don't you understand that I love her just as much as I love you? She's not him, Cass. She's You!" I yelled, angry that she really believed the words she was speaking. She truly thought leaving was the right thing to do.

"Please, Blake, don't yell. Don't you see this is exactly why I left? I don't want to fight with you. You and Alyssa had the perfect marriage. You never fought. She could do no wrong in your eyes. I can never live up to that. I'm tired of trying to live up to a ghost," she sighed in defeat.

"You can't possibly be serious right now? You don't think that Alyssa and I never fought? You think it was always perfect between us?" I asked, dumbfounded by her admission. "Cass, there's no such thing as a perfect relationship. Yes, what we had was pretty damn great, but it was far from perfect."

"It doesn't matter! This whole thing with Steve is just too much! It's a sign, Blake. Can't you see that? It just doesn't matter," she said flatly.

"All right," I said, resignation in my voice. "None of this matters to you then? I don't matter? My kids don't matter? The life we were beginning to build together doesn't matter?"

"I–I didn't mean that," she sobbed. It took everything within me not to hang up the phone and take the first flight out to be with her, but I couldn't. I had to stay strong. I had to show her how much she was hurting me–hurting us.

"You may not have meant it, Cass, but you said it."

"It's for the best," she said again. "I can't live with the distance between us anymore anyways."

"I see," I said, burning a hole through the wall I'd been staring at. "You didn't think to mention this last night when we were fucking? Was that really all it was to you, Cass? A good fuck? Because it sure felt like a lot fucking more to me. In fact, if you hadn't fallen asleep, I was going to tell you that I was planning on taking a position with Rich in Detroit."

"Wait? What?" she said, suddenly interested in what I was telling her.

"It doesn't matter. You've said so yourself," I yelled, throwing her words back at her.

"But, you said we needed to talk," she said, admitting to hearing me the night before.

"So, you were awake? You heard me tell you that I loved you?" I asked.

"Yes, I mean, no. I did hear you say that we should talk, but I didn't hear the other part. I was scared that it was all too much for you, and you were leaving. Brooke told me about the position that you'd been offered at the *Post*, and I just assumed that you were taking it. I mean, why wouldn't you? It's perfect," she explained. "But, it wasn't that at all. You love me? Why didn't you bring it up in the morning?"

"Because we had a flight to catch. We had the sentencing lingering over our heads, and I didn't want that to interfere. I just wanted it to be about us," I sighed.

"Oh," she mumbled.

"Right," I said, running my fingers through my hair. "Anyways, I think I should probably go before I say something I'd regret. It's been a long day, and I need some time to process everything."

"So, that's it then?" she asked, sounding surprised.

"Yeah, I can't fight for both of us, Cass, and you've made it perfectly clear, by not only your actions today, but also last night, that you're not willing to either. Goodbye, Cass," I said, ending the call without even waiting for her response.

I may have been wrong before. That may have been the hardest goodbye.

Chapter Twenty-Two

CASSIDY

TWO WEEKS HAD passed since I'd spoken to Blake. Fortunately, since we lived miles apart, the separation wasn't apparent to Kaity. She'd asked to Facetime Blake and the kids on a few occasions, but I'd been able to tell her that they were busy and we'd call them sometime soon. Eventually I would have to tell her the truth, but for now, I wanted to protect her from the heartbreak.

Just as I was gathering my things to leave the office for the day, I heard the bells on the door jingle.

"Hello," I said, peeking my head around the corner to find both Rich and Brooke standing in my office. "Something I can help you two with? Since I already planned your wedding, I know you aren't needing my services." Since Blake and I'd split, I'd tried distancing myself from the two of them as well. I didn't want to put them in the position of picking sides, but not having my best friend to talk to was definitely taking its toll on me.

"Yeah, we need to talk. You need to sit," Brooke said, grabbing me by the wrist and leading me to my office chair.

"Please tell me this isn't an intervention," I said, rolling my eyes.

"Can't because that's exactly what this is," Rich deadpanned, shrugging his shoulders.

"I don't have time for this. I need to pick Kaity up from my parents' place."

"They know you'll be late," Brooke interjected.

"Wait. You already talked to my parents?" I questioned. "Are you all in on this?"

"Yep," Brooke said, popping her "p." "We all know what's best for you. Even if you're being too dumb to see it for yourself."

"Yeah, and what's that, oh wise one?" I said, sarcastically.

"It's been two weeks, Cass. You need to call him," Brooke said. "You're miserable. He's miserable. This has gone on long enough."

"He told me that he needed time. He hasn't called me either. Why am I sitting here getting the third degree from you two?" I yelled.

"Trust me, if we were both in D.C. then he'd be getting it from us, too," Rich promised. "He may be my best friend, but he's acting just as foolish as you are."

"Cass, he wants you to fight for him!" Brooke hollered. "If you love him as much as you say you do then why aren't you fighting?"

"I'm scared," I admitted, tears starting to flow freely.

"Scared of what? Blake hadn't given you any reason to think he'd ever leave you. Not until you royally fucked shit up, and assumed he'd blame you for Steve's mistakes. Put yourself in Blake's shoes, Cass! Can you imagine how he must've felt? Having to relive everything that day, and to do it alone because you ran," Brooke said, seriousness in her tone. "I know Steve seriously fucked with your head, but it's time to move on. Blake's a great guy. You need to give him the chance to prove it."

I sat there for a moment, stunned speechless by the truth in her words. She was right. I hadn't given Blake a fair chance. I assumed the worst, and I ran. I broke his heart before I'd given him the chance to break mine–instead hurting us both in the process.

"You're both right," I admitted. "I've been so consumed with fear that I'm living in his wife's shadow that I failed to see how much he cares about me. I need to go home and call him. I need to make this right. Now I just hope I'm not too late."

"Trust me, you're not too late," Rich assured me. "I'll be sure to fuck him up good if he acts like a fool."

"Thanks, Dick," I said, smiling for the first time in weeks. "Brookie, can you lock up for me? I need to go!"

"You know I will. We love you, Cass," she said as I slipped out the front door.

Pulling out into traffic, I reached into my purse to grab my phone. Not immediately finding it, I quickly glanced over to see it had fallen out onto the seat. Grabbing for it, I looked up just in time to see the truck I'd been following come to a sudden stop. Before I had a chance to think about what was happening, the sound of screeching brakes, and the smell of burning rubber flooded my senses before I let unconsciousness consume me.

"Kaity, Blake," I screamed, as my world suddenly went dark. A few moments passed by before I began to hear commotion around me.

"Cassidy, Cassidy," I heard a woman's voice say, as a bright light overtook the darkness. She was dressed all in white with wavy, golden blond hair, big blue eyes, and a sun-kissed complexion.

"Where am I?" I mumbled.

"Don't be frightened. I'm here with you now," the woman said, a strange familiarity about her.

"I don't–I don't understand," I said, my head beginning to pound. "Who are you?"

"I'm Alyssa Mitchell," she said. "Blake's wife. Well, his former wife, I guess you could say." As she spoke, I slowly began to remember what led me here. Reaching for my phone, brake lights, squealing tires, shattering glass–I'd been in an accident.

"Oh god, am I dead?" I asked her. "I need to see my baby girl. I can't go. Not like this."

"No, you're very much alive, but you have to fight, Cass. You have to fight to stay alive–fight for Blake. Fight harder than I did. Please, for Blake's sake, and for my children's sake as well as for Kaity. They all need you in their lives. Be the wife and mother that I can't be. He loves you, Cass. Please don't let the love we once shared affect your relationship with him. Go–go be with him. I can tell you're a good person, and I can't think of a better woman to raise my children than you," she encouraged, before quickly fading into the ethereal distance.

"Alyssa, thank you. Alyssa," I mumbled, as I tried to open my eyes.

BLAKE

GLANCING AT THE time on my computer screen, I sighed, realizing it was nearing the end of another day and still not a word from Cass. I was starting to think that it really was over between us. Just as I was thinking about giving in and calling her, the phone rang beside me.

"Hey, Hot," I said, seeing Rich's name appear on the caller ID. "What's up?"

"I wasn't sure if you'd answer. I assumed you'd be on the next plane to Michigan," he said.

"What would make you assume that?" I asked.

"Cass didn't call you? Brooke and I talked to her. She said she was going to call you," Rich said, confusion in his tone.

"Nope, I guess she must've changed her mind."

"That doesn't make any sense. She left here about twenty

minutes ago, and said she was calling you right away."

"Sorry, Man, I don't know what to tell you. I haven't talked to her in two weeks." Just as I was about to confess that I'd considered calling her, his phone buzzed with another call.

"Hold on a second, Brooke is calling. I need to take this," he said, putting me on hold. Several seconds ticked by before he returned to the line.

"Blake," he said, seriousness suddenly in his tone.

"Is everything OK?" I asked, concerned about Brooke's pregnancy. "Is it Brooke? The twins?"

"No, she's fine," he said, pausing. "It's Cass. I don't know how to tell you this, Man. Brooke just called. Cass has been in a car accident. She's been rushed to Mercy."

Without saying a word, I set the phone down beside me–the room starting to spin rapidly. This couldn't possibly be happening to me–not again. Fate must be playing a cruel, cruel joke on me. Taking a deep breath, I picked the phone back up, unable to stifle the tears that had begun to fall.

"Rich, as my friend, you need to tell me she's going to be OK. She has to be OK," I begged.

"You know I would tell you that if I could, but we both know the grim truth about these situations," he said in earnest. "You need to get on the next flight out of there. I'll be at the airport waiting for you. I'm on my way to meet Brooke at the hospital. I'll let you know as soon as I have more details on her condition."

Before leaving the office, I'd called to secure a ticket on the next flight out of D.C. Since Rich and Brooke were both in Michigan and my parents were back in New York, I had to take the kids with me. Trying to remain calm for their sake was nearly impossible.

Luckily, I'd been able to keep tabs on Cass's condition during the flight through e-mail updates from Rich. Although she hadn't regained consciousness, the doctors were "optimistically hopeful," Rich had written in his most recent message. Leaning my head back in the seat, I said a silent prayer to God, Alyssa, and really anyone above who might take pity on me and listen.

"Please let her be all right," I pleaded. "I should've never walked away from her. I need her in my life. The kids need her in their lives. We were broken until she unknowingly swooped in and fixed us."

JUST AS HE'D promised, Rich was waiting for us at the airport. Since I hadn't checked any luggage, I scooped up both kids and ran straight out of the terminal. Fastening the kids into car seats, I slid into the passenger seat next to Rich.

"I can't believe we're here doing this again," I said, swallowing back my feelings. "Has there been any change in her condition?"

"Not that I know of," he said, patting my shoulder. "Brooke said she'd let me know right away if anything changes."

Tapping my foot against the floor, I was beginning to think I could get to the hospital quicker by foot.

"Seriously, why is there so much fucking traffic?" I asked in frustration.

"Relax, we're here," he said, pulling into the parking garage. "I'll take the kids and wait in the lobby. She's in Room 213. I think her parents are in there with Brooke."

Only half-listening to what Rich said, I jumped out of the car and bolted toward the front entrance. Once inside, I was struck by the familiar stark white walls and scent of antiseptic as haunting memories flooded my mind.

Sitting at Alyssa's side, I held her hand as the monitors she'd been hooked up to started beeping and buzzing. Immediately, I heard a "Code Blue" come through the hospital's loud speakers. It felt like someone had kicked me repeatedly in the stomach as I saw the code team rush into her room, pushing me out the door.

"She's flatlining!" I heard through the partially-closed door as I watched them begin CPR and administer medication to try and restart her heart. The room was silent as the doctors and nurses skillfully worked with a defibrillator to resuscitate my wife. I said a silent prayer as my eyes became fixed on the little green line dancing across the monitor. After what seemed like an eternity, the lead doctor finally stopped compressions, and glanced toward the clock on the wall.

"I'm calling it. Time of death 8:11 a.m.," he said. Those are the last words I remember hearing before my world crashed down around me and the fog thickened.

"Sir, can I help you with something?" the receptionist asked as I approached the desk.

"Yes, I'm looking for room 213. My girlfriend was in an accident earlier in the evening. Well, she was my girlfriend. I'm not so sure anymore. I just–I just need to see her," I said, realizing I'd just unloaded a lot more information than was necessary.

"Of course, Sir. What's her name? I can make sure she's still in that room" the receptionist said, nodding in understanding.

"Cassidy Carpenter," I said, tapping my fingers on the desk.

"Yes, she's still in room 213. Take the elevator to the second floor and make a right."

"Thank you," I said, running toward the bank of elevators.

Exiting the elevator, I turned to see Brooke and Cass's parents standing outside her door. Fearing the worst, I dashed down the hallway as quickly as possible.

"What's happening," I asked, as I approached the three of them.

"Blake! Thank god you're here!" Brooke said, wrapping her arms around me in an embrace.

"I got here as soon as I could. Why are you all out here? Is something wrong?" I asked again, hoping someone would fill me in on Cass's condition.

"Oh! You don't know?" Brooke said, sounding surprised.

"Of course I don't know. I just got here. How would I know what's going on? Last I knew, she was still unconscious. Has that changed?" I nearly shrieked, raising my brows.

"Oh, yes! I texted Rich, but he must've still had his ringer off. Cass is awake. She's a little groggy, but the doctor has already seen her. He expects her to make a full recovery. She has a nurse in there with her now. She woke up bitching, in typical Cass-like fashion, that she had to pee like a racehorse," Brooke laughed, relief in her voice.

Breathing a sigh of relief, I slowly opened the door to Cass's room. Hearing her talking to the nurse as I entered was like music to my ears.

"Well, look who finally decided to show up," she sassed, giving me a half-smile.

"I'll leave you two alone," the nurse said. "Cassidy, if you need me for anything else, please press the pager button," she added, exiting the room.

"Thanks, Donna," Cass said, as the door closed.

We stared at each other in silence for a few moments, neither of us quite knowing where to begin.

"You know, you could've just called and asked me to come. You didn't have to take such drastic measures," I said, trying to lighten the mood between us.

"Yeah, I know," she laughed. "I was actually trying to call you when all this happened. Turns out, distracted driving is a real thing. I don't suggest trying it—ever."

"Yeah, well, I'm just glad you're OK," I admitted.

"Yeah, me too. Also, turns out, ass-packing someone isn't as fun as I always thought it might be," she said, the corner of her mouth curling.

"Well, I can see the accident didn't cause any brain damage. You're still crazy as ever," I joked.

"Yeah, nothing too serious. I have a mild concussion, but the doctor said with a little rest I should be as good as new in a few weeks," she said. "They're keeping me overnight for observation, but I should be able to go home sometime tomorrow."

"Well, I'm just glad you're OK," I said, kissing her on the forehead. "I think you were trying to give me a heart attack."

"I really am sorry. I didn't mean for any of this to happen," she said. I knew she was talking about more than just the accident, but I let her continue anyways.

"Brooke and Rich helped me see what an idiot I've been. And, then, Alyssa," she paused, looking me in the eyes.

"I don't follow? What does Alyssa have to do with this?"

"I must've passed out for a minute after the crash. She came to me. I saw her, Blake. She told me to fight for you. So, this is me, fighting for you, asking you to forgive me. I love you, Mitchell," she confessed.

A smile formed on my lips, thankful for whoever helped Cass see the light. "I love you, too, Carpenter," I said, drawing her in for a tender kiss. "And, just so you know, I would've given in after three weeks, but luckily for me, you caved after just two," I added with a wink.

Chapter Twenty-Three

*A*FTER SPENDING JUST one night in the hospital, I was ready to sleep in my own bed, under my own plush, down comforter. Blake never left my side since he'd arrived the day before. I had to practically beg him to go get something to eat. I think the only reason he'd finally agreed is because I convinced him I needed something other than nasty hospital food.

Rich and Brooke had taken the kids back to their place shortly after Blake had arrived. They'd even agreed to keep them an extra night to give us a bit more privacy at home. I wasn't sure what I'd have to owe them for the favor, but at that point, I didn't really care.

"I think I'm going to go take a shower. Do you want to join me?" I asked, walking into the house.

"As much as I love the sound of that, I really don't think that's a good idea. You're supposed to take it easy, remember," he reminded me.

"But, don't you remember how much fun it was the last time I was your patient," I pouted.

Groaning, he readjusted his cock, before answering. "Yeah,

I'll never forget, but this is a little more serious, Cass. You have a head injury. We're not taking any chances. Got it," he instructed.

"Fine," I sighed. "Will you at least come and cuddle with me once I'm done? I just want to lie in my own bed."

"Now that sounds perfect," he said, placing his hands on each side of my face and kissing the top of my head, before I retreated into the bathroom.

After washing the hospital scent off my skin, I dried off and wrapped myself tightly in the towel before returning to the bedroom. Reclining on the bed, I propped myself up with several pillows.

"I called the doctor, he said light activity should be fine," I said, as Blake entered the bedroom.

"You just called the doctor now?" he asked, suspiciously.

"Mmmhmm," I responded seductively, playing with the knot which secured my towel.

"Doesn't matter, I don't think sex qualifies as 'light activity,'" he said, raising a brow.

"I specifically asked," I smirked.

"You did not call the doctor to ask if sex was an approved activity."

"I did, too! Call him and ask for yourself if you don't believe me!" I said, handing over my phone.

"I don't believe you, and I'm not going to call your doctor and ask him if I can fuck you tonight. That would just make me look like a douchebag," he said.

"Please, you don't have to fuck my brains out, or bang my head against any walls, just nice and slow?" I nearly begged, letting the towel fall open, my knees slightly open. "My pussy misses you."

Blake's jaw nearly hit the ground when he saw I wasn't wearing anything under the towel. "Fuck me," he hissed. "Carpenter, you aren't playing fair."

"You know what they say–all's fair in love and war, Mitchell."

"You always get your way, don't you?" he said, desire burning in his dark eyes.

"I don't know. Take your clothes off and find out," I teased. Without having to ask him twice, Blake ripped his T-shirt over his head in a single motion. His "V" taunting me as he slowly unzipped his jeans. Stepping out of his jeans and boxer briefs, he kneeled on the edge of the bed, his fully-erect cock already glistening with precum.

"Let me suck it," I nearly begged.

"Not tonight. As much as I'd love nothing more than to fuck your dirty, little mouth, I definitely don't think that's on your list of approved activities," he said, in a husky voice.

"No? Then why don't you show me what is approved," I suggested, motioning for him to come closer.

Pulling me down the bed closer to him, Blake didn't waste any time, using his rough hands to spread my legs further apart. Blake hovered over my core for a moment, his warm breath tickling my thighs.

"Please, Blake," I begged.

After teasing me for a few seconds longer, he brought his mouth to my lips parting my pussy with a flick of the tongue.

"Fuck, I've missed you," he growled, as he began sucking on my clit. Just when I thought I couldn't endure any more pressure, Blake plunged two fingers into my pulsating center.

"Not yet," he instructed, removing his mouth from my clit, as he scooted up higher on the bed.

"Do you want a taste?" he asked, offering me his soaked fingers.

"Mmmhmm," I moaned, not taking my eyes of him.

Gently inserting a finger in my mouth, I sucked it like I would've sucked his dick, making sure to pay close attention to the tip as I slowly swirled my tongue around it, lapping up my juices.

"You think you're cute, huh? I know what you're trying to do, Carpenter. I think you need to be punished," he said, as I felt the tip of his cock at my entrance.

"Fuck, please punish me then," I said, unable to withstand the tension building in my core.

Moaning at his sudden entrance, Blake began rocking his hips, filling me deeply with each thrust. I moved with him in complete synchronization. We knew every intimate detail of each other's bodies. Knowing what I needed to come undone, Blake brought his fingers to my clit and began rubbing them in a circular motion, causing friction to build between us.

"Fuck. Me." I mewled as an orgasm rippled through my body.

Blake pumped into me a few more times as my pussy clenched around his hardened length. He let out a guttural moan as he let out his own release. Coming down from our orgasmic high, he held me for a few minutes before either of us said a word.

"Mmmm, I'm glad I convinced you to do that," I said, already half-asleep. "I think I like you here in my bed."

"Yeah? I'm glad because that's something I'd like to talk to you about," he confessed. "I'd like to try this the right way–the way it should've been since the beginning. I know after these last two weeks that I can't live without you in my life."

"Yeah? What are you saying?" I questioned.

"I want to be with you, Cass. The kids and I are moving here to be with you and Kaity."

"What? When?" I asked. "What about your new position?"

"I resigned on my way out. Rich said the position here is still mine if I want it. I'll be here for good within the month. Honestly, if it weren't for my things, I'd never go back to D.C.," he said, matter-of-factly.

"Wow, really?" I said. "I hoped we'd be together eventually, but I didn't think it'd be this soon."

He paused for a moment, obviously surprised by my response. "Do you not want me–my kids–here? Do you not want us to be a family?"

I did want that. In fact, before everything happened with Steve and then my accident, I wanted to tell him the exact same thing. Why was I questioning everything all over again? Blake wasn't Steve. I had to stop comparing him to the douche who left me alone and pregnant. Blake wanted me and my daughter. He wanted us all to be a family.

I took a deep breath, knowing I had to be vulnerable and tell him how I felt. "I do want you here, Blake. I want you all here. I hope that someday we will all be a family. I'm just scared," I confessed, hoping he'd understand without having to further explain.

"I'm scared, too, Cass. I've only ever loved one other woman, but because of that I know what love should be like, and I know I love you. I'm ready to see where this goes. I've put some feelers out about a place. I think it'd be best to live apart for a while anyways. I want to get the kids used to the idea of us as a family before we throw them all together in one house. I hope you agree."

Wow, he was definitely very serious. "Yes, I think that's best, too," I agreed.

"Good, I'm glad it's settled then. Now, we should get some rest. You've had a long day," he said, kissing me on the tip of my nose before pulling me into his side.

Chapter Twenty-Four

CASSIDY

NEARLY SIX WEEKS had passed since Blake had moved to Michigan. He'd found a small house to rent just a few blocks from mine. It was the typical bachelor pad, I'd always envisioned him living in–white walls, and wood floors, with a black leather sectional. Honestly, I wasn't sure why he even bothered since he and the kids spent practically every night at my place anyways, but he kept insisting, saying that he didn't want to pressure me into anything.

Although I'd been lucky and didn't have any lasting side effects from the accident, I did have to take a few weeks off from work, per the doctor's orders, to fully recover from the concussion.

Since it was the height of the wedding season, I'd been swamped after my return and spent many late hours with my brides at various appointments. My favorite were always the cake-testing appointments even though my hips hadn't been agreeing with me lately, and I hadn't had much extra time to hit the gym.

"I can't decide between the pink orchids or the purple calla lilies. Oh, Mom, look at these gardenias!" my soon-to-be-bride, Kendra, squealed as she flipped through the hundredth bouquet catalog.

Taking a sip of water, I blew out a deep breath to try and calm my queasy stomach. I'd eaten a greasy patty melt and French fries for lunch and they obviously weren't settling well. Pinching the bridge of my nose, I said a silent prayer that my bridezilla would come to a decision, hopefully sometime soon. We'd already spent the entire morning trying to select a menu with a caterer, and now we'd been with the florist for the last two hours.

"Kendra, I'll be back in a few. I need to run to the ladies' room. Please feel free to make a decision without me," I encouraged, excusing myself.

I'd just made it to the sink when I lost the entire contents of my stomach. Leaning against the counter, I lifted my head and caught a glimpse of my reflection in the mirror. My complexion was chalky-white, and sweat dripped off my brow. I needed to get home, and fast. Rinsing out the sink, I splashed some water on my face in hopes of making myself somewhat presentable.

"Cassidy, are you OK, dear?" Mrs. Jacobs asked as I walked back toward the two of them.

"Actually, I'm not feeling very well. I think I must've eaten something that didn't agree at lunch," I explained.

"That's strange. We ate the same thing and I'm feeling fine," Kendra said. "Maybe you're pregnant!"

"Ha! That's a good one," I laughed. "Definitely not pregnant, but maybe I am coming down with something," I added, feeling the beginning of a dull headache.

"Oh no! You don't have the flu, do you? My girlfriends from college are flying in this weekend for my bachelorette party! I can't get sick!" Kendra yelled.

"Relax, Ken. I think you'll be fine. If Cassidy thinks it's just something she ate then I'm sure that's all it is," Mrs. Jacobs added, rubbing her daughter's shoulders. I'd had several bridezillas throughout the years, but this one was really the icing on the cake—as we liked to say in the bridal biz. "But, just to be safe, you really should be going, dear. We'll call you in the morning with our final selection."

"Thank you, ladies," I said, as they both refused my outstretched hand.

Making it to my car without incident, I dialed Brooke before pulling out into traffic.

"Hey, Cass, are we still on for the movies tonight?" she asked, as she answered the call. "I guess the guys were planning on hitting the gym after work."

"Actually, that's why I'm calling. I must've eaten something bad at lunch. I had to leave my bride and her mother at the flower shop because I hurled in the bathroom," I said, suddenly feeling another wave of nausea come on. "Hold on," I said, pulling over onto a side street.

"Cass, are you OK?" I heard Brooke ask through the Bluetooth as I puked up round two on the sidewalk. Hoping no one saw me, I quickly closed the car door and pulled back into traffic.

"Sorry," I said weakly.

"Well that was disgusting," she laughed.

"You'll live. I'm sure you've seen me do far worse. Besides, if you think that was disgusting, how are you going to handle changing poopy diapers in a few months?" I asked with a laugh.

"Oh, I thought I'd just call you each time the girls needed to be changed," she joked.

"Yeah, my years of diaper duty have long passed," I said.

"Are you sure about that?" Brooke questioned. "You're not pregnant, are you?"

"Um, yeah, I'm positive. Why does everyone keep asking me that? You know my baby factory is closed for business. I'm on the pill, and Blake and I have been super careful. I've even made him double-wrap it before."

"Dear lord, please tell me that's a lie," she giggled.

"Yeah, I couldn't do that to him. He likes the sensation of my love canal too much for that," I chuckled.

"I'm hanging up on you, right now. You didn't just call your vagina a love canal," she laughed.

"I did, but I don't think it's any worse than you calling it a vagina!"

"Um, that's what it is!" Brooke yelled through the phone.

"You're so damn prim and proper sometimes. It's a pussy, Brookie. Pussy. Say it with me, Puss–see!" I teased.

"You're ridiculous, I'm ignoring you because I'm trying to be serious here. Are you late?" Brooke asked, in a much more serious tone.

"Late? Late for what? What the fuck are you talking about?" I responded, trying to ignore my rumbling stomach.

"Your period, dumbass. Are you late?"

Thinking back, I tried using my fingers to count back to my last period. "Fuck, I don't know," I screamed. "Maybe. Fuck."

"Calm down, you're still driving. You need to pull over and take some deep breaths," Brooke suggested. "We don't need you to end up in the hospital again."

"No, what I need to do is drive to the fucking pharmacy and buy a fucking pregnancy test," I said, panic beginning to set in. I really was late—at least ten days late. I'd only even been late one other time in my life–and nine months later I was a mother.

ARRIVING HOME, I immediately ran into the bathroom to empty my stomach for the third time. I wasn't even sure how there was anything left in it at this point. Sitting on the cold linoleum floor, I stared at the unopened box in my hand. If I was, in fact, pregnant, I had no idea how I was going to tell Blake. How would he even react? The last time I'd been in this position, in this same exact room, my relationship had crumbled before my very eyes. The only difference between then and now is that I didn't love Steve. Sure, I was hurt when he left me, but I was able to move on. If Blake left, I wasn't sure if I'd ever recover. After all, I'd hardly survived for the few weeks we had been apart.

We'd never talked about having children together. I didn't know if he wanted more kids five or ten years from now, let alone in nine months. Fuck, together, we'd have four kids all under the age of six. And, what if the unimaginable happened and I was knocked up with twins like Brooke. I wasn't even sure if they made strollers and minivans big enough for that many kids.

Just as I was getting up the nerve to go and pee on the stick, the door swung open without so much as a knock.

"Whoa, Kaity, you know better than to barge into the bathroom," I said, not taking my eyes from the same tile I'd been staring at for the last fifteen minutes.

"It's not Kaity," Blake said as I looked up from the floor.

"Oh, hey," I said, tucking the pregnancy test under my leg. "I thought you were going to the gym with Rich."

"Brooke told me that I probably should come here first to check on you. I knocked, but you obviously didn't answer. So, I used my key," he said, dangling it in the air. "You don't look so good. Everything all right?"

The rational side of my brain was telling me to tell Blake the truth; That he would understand, and be the most amazing father to our child. He'd been furious with me when I doubted him, and our relationship before. I knew I wouldn't be able to keep this secret from him much longer. But, the irrational side was toying with my emotions, telling me that Blake would walk out of my life–our lives–just as Steve had done almost six years earlier.

"Just a touch of food poisoning. Brooke really shouldn't have bothered you. Go to the gym with Rich. I'll be fine," I lied.

"Yeah? You sure about that?" he questioned, joining me on the floor.

"I'm sure," I said, nodding my head in agreement.

"Then what's in the box hiding under your leg?"

"What box?" I said, picking up my left leg. "I don't see a box."

"Your right leg, Cass. I'm not dumb," he said, raising his brows.

Swallowing the lump that had lodged in my throat, I finally opted to tell Blake the truth–praying that he would stay here with me, and not walk out the door. "It's a pregnancy test," I said, my eyes brimming with tears.

"You're pregnant?" he asked in an even tone.

"I don't know," I answered, shrugging my shoulders. "I haven't taken the test yet. I guess I'm too scared to do it."

"Why? I don't understand," he said, shaking his head in confusion. "You don't want another baby–my baby?"

"It's not that. We–we just haven't talked about more kids. And, the last time," I stopped, wiping the tears from my eyes.

"Cass, look at me," Blake said, placing his finger on my chin. "Since I truly believe you aren't thinking clearly right now, I'm going to pretend you didn't suggest that I'm anything like Steve. Especially considering everything that we've recently overcome. Fight for us, Baby."

"I'm sor—," I interrupted.

"Shhh, I'm not finished," he added, moving his finger to my lips. "It's true that we haven't talked about having children, but that doesn't, for a minute, mean that I don't think about having babies with you–everyday. I can't think of anything better than for you to be pregnant with my child."

"Really?" I asked, the corners of my mouth turning up.

"Really," he said, bringing my head down to rest on his firm chest. "Well, I can think of one thing better."

Exhaling sharply, I knew it was too good to be true. "What's that?" I asked.

"Well, I'd ask you to be my wife, but I don't want you to assume I'm only asking you because you may or may not be pregnant. So, just know that I do want you to be my wife, Carpenter, and I will ask you again–whether it be tomorrow, next week, or five years from now," he confessed. "Now I think it's time I step out into the bedroom so you can pee on that stick."

Blake left the room for a few minutes as I took care of business and quickly brushed my teeth. Opening the door into the bedroom, I took a seat next to Blake on the side of the bed.

"Are you OK?" he asked, lacing his fingers with mine.

"Yeah, I'm actually not feeling too bad now," I said, shocking myself that I meant it.

"Would you be mad at me if I said I hope it's positive?" he questioned, placing a gentle kiss on my forehead.

"No, because I think I want it to be positive, too," I said, placing my other hand on my stomach.

"What are your favorite baby names–boy and girl?" Blake asked, trying to pass the time.

"I don't know. I haven't really thought about it," I admitted.

"That's why it's fun. No thinking. Just tell me what two names you come up with first."

"Hmmm," I mumbled.

"Stop! I said no thinking," he chuckled.

"OK, fine, Josie and Dominic."

"Mine are Luke and Leia."

I eyed him suspiciously before responding, "We are not naming our children after *Star Wars* characters."

Shrugging, he laughed, "At least I didn't suggest Anakin."

We sat in silence for a few more minutes, waiting for the

results. "Do you think it's time yet?" Blake asked after three minutes had passed.

"Yeah, I think so. Do you want to look, or do you want me to look?" I asked, rising from the edge of the bed.

"It's up to you," he said, standing beside me.

"You do it. I don't think I can look," I said, sitting back down.

Blake walked back into the bathroom, and quickly returned with the stick. Judging by the look on his face, I knew the results of the test before he even spoke the words.

"Well, I really wasn't expecting that," I said, glancing at the ceiling. "I guess it really was just some indigestion."

"One day it'll be positive, Baby. You can bet on that," he said, walking up to the bed and pulling my head into his chest. He stroked the back of my head for several minutes as I cried into his shirt for the child we'd lost, yet I'd never even carried.

Chapter Twenty-Five

CASSIDY ~ *Six weeks later*

AFTER MEETING WITH clients for most of the afternoon and early evening, I'd been dreaming of coming home, slipping into my favorite yoga pants, and lounging on the couch while eating an entire carton of Ben and Jerry's. With Blake's parents coming to town for a visit, I wasn't planning on seeing him after work. Instead we'd made plans for the following evening. Gathering my things, my phone suddenly rang in my purse. Digging through all my junk, I found it just before it went to voicemail.

"Hey," I said, answering the call. "Did your parents get in?"

"Well, that's actually why I'm calling," he said. "Their flight out was canceled and they won't be arriving until morning. Do you want to get dinner? I was thinking that new place we've been eyeing would be good. Brooke said she'd watch the kids for us."

"But, I've been dreaming all day about yoga pants, the TV, and Ben and Jerry's," I pouted.

"You better be talking about the ice cream," he deadpanned.

"Um, yeah, it's delicious," I said, fluttering my eyes and moaning.

"OK, so scratch dinner out then. How about I just bring the

kids over and we can grab a pizza and eat ice cream? Especially if you're going to moan like that while you're eating it."

"And you, Mitchell, really are the perfect man."

"I know, but do me a favor and remember that the next time I fuck up," he laughed.

"Mmmhmmm," I agreed.

"Good enough for me. I'll see you in twenty. Love you, Carpenter."

"Love you, too," I responded, ending the call.

AS I LOUNGED on the couch, watching Maddy and Ben play, waiting for Blake to bring me a big, heaping bowl of Ben and Jerry's, Kaity ran out into the living room from the kitchen where she'd been helping scoop the ice cream.

"Mommy, can you be Maddy and Ben's mommy, too?" she asked out of nowhere.

"Kaity, Baby, where did that idea come from," I asked, looking over toward Blake who'd entered the room and taken sudden interest in the conversation. "Brendan has both a mommy and a daddy. I just wondered if Maddy and Ben could have you as their mommy so they'd have both a mommy and a daddy, too."

I took a minute before I could answer my daughter. How was I about to explain death to her? I knew the day would come eventually, but I wasn't at all prepared for it today. Truthfully, I had dreamed of Kaity calling Blake, Dad. She'd never had a daddy to read her a bedtime story, sit with her when she had a fever, or rock her to sleep after a nightmare. But, Maddy and Ben—they had a mother. A mother who loved them as a mother should. She had dreams and aspirations for them. I could never replace her. I knew I loved them as my own, but I'd already made the decision that I would always remain Cass.

"They do have a mommy, Baby. They have a mommy in heaven who loves them very much," I said, biting the inside of my cheek and doing my best not to cry.

Kaity looked over in Blake's direction and then back at me before responding. I could almost see the little wheels working overtime in her head. "OK, well if they already have a mommy . . . can Blake be my daddy? I don't have a daddy here or in heaven," she reminded me.

"Kaity, I don't think . . ."

Blake stopped me mid-sentence as he slid on the couch, sandwiching Kaity between the two of us.

"Kaity, I would be honored if you called me, Daddy," he told her, running his fingers through her fine blond hair.

"And, you, Cassidy, I would be even more honored if you allowed my children to call you 'Mommy.' It's true, they will always have a mother watching over them from heaven, but they need a mother here on earth, too."

I shook my head. Not because I wanted to tell him no, but because I was in disbelief. From the moment I met Blake Mitchell, I knew he was different, but even after all this time, he still somehow managed to keep surprising me.

"I don't know what to say," I said, taking a deep breath.

"Just say 'yes,'" he said, reaching into his pocket.

"What?" I asked. Noticing the big smile that had appeared on my daughter's face.

"Cassidy Leigh Carpenter, will you be my wife?" he asked, sliding down onto one knee.

"Did you two set me up?" I asked Kaity.

She shrugged her tiny shoulders before responding. "Say yes, Mommy. Say yes!" she squealed, as all of the kids began clapping their tiny hands together.

Before I had too much time to think, I blurted out my answer.

"Yes, yes, I'll marry you!" I nearly shouted, falling into his arms and bringing Kaity down with me. The smile on his face and the gleam in his eyes assured me that I'd made the right decision.

"I still can't believe you put her up to this," I said, unable to wipe the huge grin from my face.

"Well it didn't exactly happen that way," he began to explain. "I was planning on asking you to marry me at dinner tonight, but then Kaity came to me with her questions earlier today while you were at work. I told her they were things she should probably discuss with you. I decided then that this should be a family affair, and that I wanted to ask you to be my wife now, instead of waiting until we were alone."

"May I be excused?" Kaity asked, wiggling out of our embrace.

I chuckled, realizing I'd forgotten Kaity was still sandwiched between us.

"Sorry, Baby. You can go," I said, sitting back.

Before she ran off, Blake grabbed her arm. "Actually, Kaity, before you go, I have something for you, too."

Surprising us both, Blake reached into his other pocket, and pulled out a charming necklace and pendant–something fit for a princess.

"I wanted to make sure this was OK with you too, Kaity. Is it OK if I marry your mommy? Can I be your Daddy?" he said, looking at her as if she were the only person in the room. The tears I'd been able to hold back when he asked me to marry him were now streaming down my cheeks.

She looked at me first as if asking for my permission to give Blake her answer.

"Go ahead," I mouthed, nodding my head.

"Yes, it's OK if you marry my mommy, Daddy," she said, smiling up at him.

Sitting back on the couch, Blake pulled me toward him, searing my lips with a kiss. "Just so you know, I intend on making this official. I want to legally adopt Kaity. As long as you agree, of course," he said, in an extremely serious tone.

"Of course it's fine with me. I can't think of a better man than you to help me raise my daughter."

"I'm glad you agree. And, I'd also like you to adopt my children. I know that life can change in the blink of an eye, and I just want to know that if something ever happens to me that they'll have a mother who'll love them and care for them unconditionally. I know you're that woman, Cass."

"Truthfully, in my heart, they're already my children. I'd be honored to make it official," I said, leaning into him.

"This night turned out pretty damn perfect," he said, peppering kisses on my neck.

"I can only think of one thing that would make it better," I responded.

"When the kids go to bed," he whispered, his trail of kisses extending down to my collarbone.

"Mmmhmm, but I was actually referring to the Ben & Jerry's," I quipped.

Chapter Twenty-Six

BLAKE ~ *Six months later*

$\mathcal{L}$ OOKING IN THE mirror, I readjusted my tie for what seemed like the billionth time. I'd been here before, but this time seemed just a little different. Maybe it was because we'd already overcome so many obstacles that eventually led us to this day, or maybe it's because I now know that I can't take anything in life for granted.

Hearing a light rap on the door, I yelled, "Come in," assuming it was Rich.

"Hey, Man. Are you doing OK?" he asked, handing me a wrapped package. "Your bride asked me to give this to you."

"Yeah, I'm feeling all right. Just the few expected jitters," I admitted.

"Do you want me to drive the getaway car? It's still not too late, you know?"

"You better not hope I tell Cass you said that. I think she and your wife would kill you," I chortled.

"Cass might, but I think Brooke needs me too much with all these kids running around," he laughed. "Besides, you know I love Cass like a sister. Just don't go telling her I said that shit."

"Your secret is safe with me, Hot. And, stop your whining

about the kids, Cass and I have just as many running around," I said, patting him on the back.

"Not for much longer," he grumbled.

"Wait? What are you saying? Is Brooke pregnant again?" I asked.

"Yeah, we were going to wait to tell you two because today is about you, but I seriously need to tell someone. We found out yesterday that she's indeed pregnant again. Thankfully, although I love my twins to death, there was only one heartbeat this time," he said.

"You know you can wrap that shit, right?" I joked. "The girls are what, like four-months-old?"

"Yeah, well, Brooke's doctor didn't think that even with the healthy pregnancy that she'd be able to conceive again with her history of endometriosis so we didn't really worry about it. Once we were given the all-clear after six weeks, well I just went for it," he said. "We tried for years and now it's like I simply look at her and bam–pregnant."

"Well, I didn't see that one coming at all. Congrats, Hot," I said. "You two are going to be the fucking Waltons before you know it."

Shaking his head, he said, "I have a feeling she's going to make me get my junk snipped before we're raising our own fucking baseball team."

"Shit. Sorry, Dude. I'd rather not even think about scissors near my family jewels," I said, reaching down to adjust my junk.

"Yeah, well, enough about me and my super sperm. Let's go get you married," he laughed, patting me on the back.

"Right, but first I think I'd like to open this gift in private–in case Cass decided to give me some nude pictures or something."

"She didn't, I already looked," he said, a shit-eating-grin appearing on his face.

"You're such a fucker," I joked, as Rich exited the room.

Tearing off the letter attached to the box, I opened it first.

Mitchell,

I can't believe this day has come. Thank you for believing in us and believing in me. Thank you for continuing to fight when I'd forgotten how. And, thank you for allowing me to see that fairy tales really do exist.

I usually tell my brides to create a scrapbook as a gift to their groom with all the memories they've shared together. So, I thought I'd take my own advice and make one for you–for us. I love you, Blake Thomas Mitchell.

Always,

Carpenter–Soon-to-be-Mitchell

Opening the scrapbook, I flipped through the pages of pictures of us with the kids–a selfie of us sledding on your first "play date," a picture of the girls with Olaf their snowman, as well as the plane ticket stubs from her trip to New York. She'd kept it all.

Nearing the end of the book, I stopped, not recognizing the copied certificates that she'd placed there. Reading the words, I realized we'd received official documentation of both my adoption of Kaitlyn and Cass's adoption of Maddy and Ben. In the eyes of the law, I was officially Kaitlyn's father, and Cass was Maddy's and Ben's mother. And, as once as we said, "I do," we'd all officially become a family.

CASSIDY

I'D GIVEN THE same pep talk to hundreds of my brides trying to calm their nerves as they prepared to make their descent down the aisle. For some reason, it always seemed better when

I wasn't the one on the receiving end. "He loves you, Cass, and more importantly, you love him. Keep your eyes on the prize," I whispered to myself, as I stood in front of a whirling fan trying not to overheat.

"Do you need anything? It's about that time," Brooke said, coming up behind me.

"No, I'm good–perfect actually," I said, a smile forming on my lips. "Let's do this."

Keeping our ceremony relatively small, we'd only invited our immediate family and closest friends. My life was so consumed with planning everyone else's extravagant wedding that I just wanted my own to remain small and intimate.

Standing at the altar in a fitted, cream satin gown with my handsome groom standing across from me, I smiled as the pastor called our children up to join us for a special surprise that I knew they'd love. As they approached us, they were each handed a small jar filled with a different color of sand.

"Cassidy and Blake, today you're making a commitment to share the rest of your lives with each other as a family. Your relationship is symbolized through the pouring of these individual containers of sand, one representing Cassidy, one representing Blake, and the other three representing your children," the pastor said, reciting from a script. "By blending this sand together, you're unifying yourselves and your children as one family."

"Do you agree to make this commitment to each other and your children?" the pastor asked.

Smiling at each other, we spoke in unison. "We do."

Each of us poured our sand into the larger vase before the kids dumped theirs into it as well.

"In time, I hope that you choose to add additional layers of sand by making the decision to grow your beautiful family," the pastor continued, as I looked over at Blake, placing a hand on my stomach.

After repeating our vows, and exchanging rings, the pastor officially united us as man and wife, and made the announcement we'd been waiting the entire ceremony to hear.

"Blake, you may kiss your bride," he said.

Blake tipped me back in dramatic fashion, and placed a lingering kiss on my lips. Before lifting me, he whispered in my ear. "Were you trying to tell me something earlier when the pastor mentioned us growing our family?"

"Yeah, I took a test earlier this morning–it had two pink lines this time." I said slyly.

"You're pregnant?" he asked, so only I could hear.

"I'm pregnant," I confirmed, a wide smile on my lips.

"I don't know how you did it, but you made an already perfect day even more perfect," he said, kissing me again. "I love you, Carpenter-now-Mitchell."

"And, I love you, too, Mitchell."

Epilogue

"**M**OM! MADDY WON'T get out of the bathroom, and I need to finish getting ready!" I shouted, pounding on the bathroom door that I shared with my younger sister. "Maddy, get out, please! Dylan is going to be here soon, and I still haven't done my hair!" I'd been dating Dylan Christensen, the star quarterback of the varsity football team, for the last three months, and tonight, I hoped, he was going to officially ask me to go steady.

"You were already in here for forty minutes," Maddy protested. "Dad is taking Ben and me to the movies once he gets home. I'm supposed to meet Brendan there!" she yelled through the door.

"Ugh! I don't even know how you can stand that kid. He's such a pest. If you ask me, you can do so much better, Maddy," I shot back.

"Well, good thing I didn't ask you then, isn't it," she said, poking her head around the door. "I still want to marry him someday," she sighed, dreamily.

Using the small gap to my advantage, I pushed myself through the doorway, right past her.

"Hey, thanks, Sis," I said, yanking the already hot curling

iron from her hand. "And, you better not let Dad hear you say that–ever."

"You're such an asshole," she sassed, rolling her eyes.

"Mom! Maddy called me an asshole," I yelled, smirking over my shoulder at her.

"Seriously, do you two ever stop? And, Maddy, don't call your sister an asshole–even if she's being one," Mom said, as she carried a load of laundry from the baby's room. "Oh, and Maddy, Dad called and said he and the boys are running late–something about soccer practice going longer than expected," Mom added, as my six-month-old sister, Josie, began crying in her crib.

Even though Mom would never admit it, I knew Josie was a big "oops." Mom and Dad were both in their early forties and were looking forward to the days when all of us would finally be off to college and out of the house when along came an unexpected surprise. The younger kids didn't know, but I knew Mom made Dad go and have a little "procedure" after she was born.

"Would one of you get your sister, please? I need to get dinner in the oven. I promised your Aunt Brooke some girl time while you asshole kids, whom I love so dearly, are gone for the night. She's bringing the wine, but left the cooking up to me–Lord knows after all these years, she's still the only person I know who can burn a hot dog."

"I got her," I said, curling my last strand of hair. "Bathroom is all yours, Madeline."

"Ahhhh! You know I hate it when you call me that," she pouted, stomping back into the bathroom and slamming the door.

"Hey! What have I told you kids about slamming doors," Dad shouted, walking into the house with my brothers, Ben and Luke.

"Sorry, Daddy," Maddy said, coming out of the bathroom and flinging herself into Dad's arms. She'd always been his perfect little angel. "Can we go now?"

"Actually, Uncle Rich is going to take you. He said he'd be here shortly.

"Hey, Mitchell," Mom said, walking into the living room.

"Hey, yourself, Mitchell. I missed you," Dad replied, pulling her in for a kiss–just like he had every night for the past twelve years.

"Yuck! You two are so gross," Luke said, after plopping down on the couch and flipping on cartoons.

"Yeah, are you two ever going to stop?" I asked, already knowing the answer.

"Um, nope. And, if any of you don't like it, you know where your rooms are," Dad joked, pulling Mom in for another kiss.

Rolling my eyes, I sighed knowing this was just a typical day in the Mitchell household.

Acknowledgements

FIRST AND FOREMOST, I want to thank my readers—you amaze me every single day. Without you, I wouldn't have continued on this writing journey. Your daily messages are the highlight of many of my days. The friendships I have made with many of you, I know will last a lifetime. For that I'm truly grateful. I've said it before and I'll say it again, there are so many wonderful books to choose from and I'm truly honored that you took the time to read mine. Thank you for the bottom of my heart!

To my beta readers: Johnaka McCosker, Tammi Hart, Shannon Mummey, and Katie Monson—thank you for helping me dig deeper and making Unforeseen a much more polished story. You answered my unending questions and in the process have become some of my dearest friends. Thank you and I love you all more than you will ever know!

To Angie: My real-life Cassidy; Thank you for providing Cass's sass and sarcasm. Without you, she definitely wouldn't be the same.

To Julie Monaco: You've been my girl since DAY ONE! I love your face more than you will ever know! Thank you for talking me off the ledge on more than one occasion and for sending me goofy Snaps even though I can't figure out how to return them! I can't wait to squeeze you again my van chasing, Juicy Jules!

To Christina Rhoads: Thank you for just being you. Thank you for going "drunk" live with me, even though it was out of your comfort zone, just because I thought it'd be fun. Thank you for loving my stories and my characters more than I think I even do at times–and for answering my unending PMs to answer my timeline questions. Thank you for reminding me why I write the stories in my head. I could go on and on, but just know you are a truly special person and deserve the very best out of life–don't ever think otherwise . . . EVER! I love you! #BlakeIsYours

Christina Gipson: Thank you for not thinking I was a crazy stalker when I PM'd you to tell you we lived within a mile of each other. I've had so much fun over the last year with you on our crazy adventures. I didn't think it was actually possible to talk for six hours straight during a road trip, but we managed to do it–there and back! I can't wait for more road trips, fast food horror stories, movies, concerts, and chats with you! #NoBitch

To Rhonda James: Thank you for cracking the whip! I don't think I could've typed the last 40K words without you in my corner! You're my sprinting partner for life–just remember, those are only word sprints because the only time I'll sprint for real is if a bear is chasing me! Love you, Lady! Now, I think you said something about a drink!?!?!

To my Nachos: Gia Riley and Mandi Beck—thank you for keeping me "somewhat" sane and for really just being you. I would be lost in this world without you.

Jillian Toth: Jilly Bean, who would've thought when we met nearly four years ago that we'd be where we are today? You and your girls have become my family. I love you tons and I'm so proud of you!

To Kristi Falteisek: Thank you for being in my corner, and helping me achieve my goals! I'm so happy that we've been able to work together on getting Unforeseen into as many readers' hands as possible!

To Kylie and staff at Give Me Books—thank you for helping

me with the behind-the-scenes work with my release blitz. You have no idea how much your support means to me.

To all of the amazing ladies who worked to beautify *Unforeseen*: my fabulous cover designer, Michele Catalano, for taking my visions and turning them into realities; Lauren Perry of Perrywinkle Photography for the beautiful cover photo—you truly are such a talent. I knew when I saw you post these photos over two years ago that your couple was my Blake and Cass. To this day, they're still my Blake and Cass; and Christine Borgford of Type A Formatting for the stunning inside formatting—thank you for always helping me in any way that you possibly can! You've been with me since the very beginning and I can't imagine this journey without you in it.

To some of the most incredible indie authors I've met during this journey–In an attempt to not miss anyone, I'll simply say you know who you are! Thank you for your stories, advice, GIF conversations, and friendship. There aren't enough words to express my appreciation. Love you all!

To the bloggers who have shared in the cover reveal, reviewed and promoted *Unforeseen*—none of this would be possible without your constant hard work and dedication. Your support humbles me on a daily basis—thank you!

To, my husband, Brian: Thank you for your "support" during my writing journey. For listening to me whine, putting up with the sink full of dishes, and the piles of unfolded laundry while I'm on deadline–and all the other times. I love you!

To my dad: Thank you and your librarian ways for showing me at a young age that books could be pretty cool. And, thank you for reading my words! You've always supported my ideas, some crazier than others, and I'll be forever grateful. I love you!

Please feel free to join my Facebook group, M.C. Decker's Books, to talk about Unforeseen as well as other books by M.C.

Decker. *www.facebook.com/groups/MCDeckersBooks*

Also, enjoy the playlist I created for Unforeseen.

https://open.spotify.com/user/12130668278/playlist/5Znihwjgq-SiKvdTS4qVu2C

About the Author

M.C. DECKER IS an international bestselling author who loves to write stories of true love and second chances. She lives in a suburb of Flint, Michigan with her husband, Brian, and spoiled-rotten Siamese cat, Simon. For the last decade, she has worked as a journalist for several community newspapers in Michigan. She enjoys all things '80s and '90s pop culture: movies, boy bands, music and especially the color, hot pink. She also strictly lives by the motto, "Life is better in flip flops," and is a diehard Detroit Tigers fan.

Also by M. C. Decker

UNSPOKEN SERIES
Unwritten
Unscripted
Unwritten & Unscripted Box Set
Unwrapped (holiday novella)

STANDALONES
Love Entwined
Forever Entwined (A Love Entwined novella)

Made in the USA
Columbia, SC
25 August 2018